Notes

Sienna Beasley

Contents

01 | Last Day

Aliyia

I don't want to move. I don't want to leave my childhood house. So many memories have been made here and now I'm being forced to leave it all behind.

I start to tear up as I pack my brown teddy bear. I smile back at it when I remember who I received it from. My childhood best friend. I'll never forget him. So many memories were made with him in this very house. One of the reasons why I wish I could stay.

I finish packing one suitcase and stand up. We are moving tomorrow. Our flight is at 6:30 am meaning we have to wake up at like 2 am. My parents like to be early for some reason.

Once my mom made us come to the airport at 11 am when our flight was at 5:25. About 6 whole hours were spent at the airport for no reason.

I've finished packing. Everything in my room is gone except for a few blankets that I will sleep on for the night and clothes I will use to sleep and travel. Every memory I've cherished in this exact room, is gone in a few hours.

We are moving to New York. It's already November meaning it's getting colder there. I've been to New York once in my life and that was during Christmas break in 7th grade.

A knock suddenly occurs on my bedroom door. My father walks in and leans on the door.

"How are you holding up kiddo?" He asks gently.

Him calling me kiddo makes me feel some sort of joy. It's been my nickname since forever so I guess that's why it brings me comfort. My old friend used to call me kiddo. He's only about a year older than me.

"I don't want to leave," I say, leaning against the built-in mirror.

"I know kiddo, but it's for the better," he says.

"Why couldn't you get a better job here?"

"Trust me, it'll give you and your sister better opportunities. And your sister already got accepted to a college there."

After a moment of silence, my dad gets the hint and leaves the room. The familiar Oregon air came flowing through my open window.

Taking a seat on the ground, I tear at all the memories I've made here. My favorite memories being with the one person who made me the happiest as a child. I don't know where he is now. He could still be in Oregon for all I know.

One sad thing is I'll probably never find out. I've already tried searching his name on social media but he's nowhere to be found. Maybe he uses an alias or some random ass name. Or he just doesn't use social media.

One thing I know about him is his love for hockey. When we were kids all he talked about was becoming a professional hockey player one day. I hate myself for forgetting his name. It's like it's in the back of my head but I can't figure out what it is.

Suddenly there's a loud knock on my door. I shout for the person to come in and I'm instantly shocked by the person I'm seeing. My childhood best friend is at my door.

He looks grumpy and is repeating something but I can't hear him. Once I blink he's gone and replaced with my older sister, Aurora. I'm hallucinating.

"Aliyia!" She shouts at me. "Hey! Get it together, and get ready we are going to the restaurant soon." Aurora speaks again before slamming my door.

She's right I do need to get it together. Now I'm hallucinating. What a freakish thing to do.

Finally getting up, I walk to my closet that only has three outfits in it. I picked up a plain white dress and walked over to my carry-on to grab my hairbrush. Then I grab a necklace from my carry-on and place it on my neck.

"Aliyia hurry up!" I hear my mother yell from downstairs.

I sigh and put on my white converse. I'm not the biggest fan of heels. Last time I wore heels I almost broke my ankle.

Grabbing my phone, and a mini white bag, I rush down the stairs to see my family standing by the door.

"Took you long enough" Aurora groans.

I roll my eyes at her and follow them out the door.

Aurora drove, my dad sat in the passenger seat beside her, and my mom and I sat in the back.

My mom placed her hand on top of mine and gave me a soft smile. "I know moving is going to be hard for you, but I'll make sure we come back to visit as much as we can."

She always finds a way to warm my heart when I'm in a bad mood. Instead of responding I return the smile to her and rest my head on her shoulder.

Not long after we reach the restaurant. It's an expensive restaurant, my parents only want us here to treat us one last time in Oregon.

The menu looked too good but the prices. $35 for fancy spaghetti on a fancy plate? Bullshit.

The dinner was amazing. We had a nice family talk about all the things we would like to do in New York. We also talked about all the good things we experienced here. Aurora started tearing up, and so did my Mom.

Good thing I wasn't the only one feeling super emotional about this.

It felt like that dinner was so short. That made everything feel worse. My last dinner in my childhood town ended like the flash.

As soon as I got home I crashed into my blankets even though it was only 7 pm. We had to wake up early anyway.

02 | New York

Aliyia

It's almost time to say a final goodbye. I'm not trying to be too dramatic about this but I am certainly emotionally attached to this place. I mean I was born here.

It's currently 2:20 PM and my parents are double checking everything. Aurora is hugging her bedroom floor. Literally.

My phone starts to go off with texts from a few of my friends here. A lot of them saying they'll miss me, have a safe flight, not to forget them, and to visit soon. Leaving all these people makes me have a fever.

New York Central High is the high school I'm transferring to. Apparently it's really big and it has a whole ass hockey rink.

I plan to join their volleyball team since it's gonna start next week. Volleyball is one of the things I love a lot. I've been playing volleyball since sixth grade.

"Aliyia its time to go, we don't want to miss our flight!" I hear my mom shout from downstairs.

Miss our flight? It's 2 AM and our flight is at 6:30.

I take one last look at my childhood room before closing the door and walking downstairs. Everyone was practically in tears.

When all our carryons and suitcases were packed in the car, I took one last look at my house while my dad drove away tears fighting their way out.

The airport was surprisingly packed. It's only 3am and there's a lot of people here. Maybe everyone is leaving their childhood home.

We've been at the airport for 2 hours and a half. Our flight is in 20 minutes. My dad bought subway for us all to eat. Subway for breakfast, yum.

15 minutes later, they start letting people board 5 minutes early. I greet the flight attendants as I'm boarding the plane, and immediately go straight to my seat.

I fought my way for the window seat. I hate and love the window seat.

One good thing about it is you get to watch sunrises and just the sky in general.

One bad thing about it is if you have to use the washroom or something, you have to push your way through the people beside you.

Once I had to sit with two strangers who were both old and deep asleep. Both their feet were blocking my way so I almost tripped on them, trying to get out.

When everyone was settled, the plane finally began to move.

As we lifted up in the air, I could see the entire city with one glance.

One stop and seven hours later, we finally arrive in New York City.

From what I saw in the air, it was very beautiful. I'm sure it would look better at night.

The airport was once again packed with people getting ready to board a plane or people exiting a plane.

I'm standing near the baggage conveyor belt while my family is scattered somewhere in the airport.

People were pushing through the crowd trying to get their luggage and everything. All I could hear was people shouting at each other.

Once I finally see our luggage, I struggle to get all of the bags. I don't understand why they're making me get all of the bags.

I meet up with them where we planned to meet up and listen in to their conversation.

My parents and Auroras vehicles don't arrive until Wednesday. It's currently Sunday meaning I have to either take a bus, call an Uber, or walk to my school until then.

I have my learners so I can take the driving test in a few months.

Our Uber arrives about 20 minutes later, and takes us to our new home.

03 | First Day

A liyia

Today is my first day at my new school. I'm really nervous.

I have social anxiety too so that clearly won't help.

It was hard enough making friends at my old school, now I have to attempt to make friends at the biggest high school in the city.

I hate Mondays.

Anyways, I get up from my set-up blanket on the ground and take a boiling hot shower.

I walked to my closet and pick out a white cropped shirt, blue baggy jeans, and a red zip-up to go on top.

Paired with black converse and silver jewelry.

All our home materials are arriving tomorrow evening, so we have to improvise with the blankets we brought.

Makeup. I don't know how I really feel about it but I do put it on a lot. It just makes me feel even more prettier than I already am.

Although I have social anxiety and all that shit, if someone really pisses me off I might just have something to say.

My backpack was just a plain black bag. I have the choice to use a tote bag or an actual backpack but considering it's my first day and who knows how much work they'll give me, I'll take my backpack.

"Aliyia we gotta go!" Aurora yells from the first floor of our new home.

"Coming" I yell back, grabbing my bag and phone.

The car ride there was just silenced. Nothing but the wind and other cars making noise. It wasn't a bad silence, as much as I hate to admit it I feel comfortable with my sister.

"You're gonna be fine, trust me" Aurora speaks as she makes a right turn.

I simply nod in return.

Aurora has to go to a brand new college too, I should comfort her but I've never really been good at comforting people. I just can never find the right words.

We pull up at the school, and I'll just say it looks way bigger than what it shows on google maps.

I feel like I'm gonna shrink seeing the people in there.

Everyone who walked by were already in friend groups so I doubt anyone would let me join theirs.

"Good luck," Aurora says as I exit the car.

"You too" I respond, shutting the car door and walking into the building.

Large ass hallways.

After checking in with the office and receiving my timetable, I make my way to my locker.

I feel like I'm in a teenage movie because there are literally two people making out right beside my locker.

Get a room.

My first period was fucking math, I literally want to kill myself.

Groaning to myself, I shut my locker and try and look for room 8.

Why the hell is this school so big?

As I scan the halls for room 8 I bump into a hard chest.

I mentally slap myself for attracting attention in less than an hour.

"Oh, my bad" a perfect voice speaks.

The person's voice was between deep and soft, just perfect.

When I look up I see the most gorgeous guy I've ever laid my eyes on. He has two different eye colors oh my gosh.

His hair is really fluffy I just want to run my fingers through it.

And don't even get me started with his outfit.

One thing about me is I'm a sucker for guys in cargo pants, it's just really hot to me.

This guy is wearing khaki cargo pants with a plain black hoodie on top.

Basic but hot.

"Uh hello, are you okay?" He asks, moving his hand back and forth in my face.

I guess I zoned out while admiring him.

"Um yeah sorry" I fixed my posture. "Um, do you know where I can find room 8? I have math rig it away and I'm new here so." I speak awkwardly.

That is definitely going to scare him away.

"Oh, you have math? Me too I'll just take you there," he says and gestures for me to follow him.

I felt weird but I'm glad he was friendly and wasn't rude.

"I'm Zayden by the way" he introduces.

"Aliyia," I say, gripping the hem of my zip-up.

As we both enter the classroom the teacher stops me from going to my seat and makes me stand in front of the entire class to introduce myself.

It was one of the most awkward experiences I've ever felt.

Some people were silently judging, I could tell by their faces and the way they whispered to their friends looking back and forth at me.

I take a seat at the back of the class and start playing with my fingers.

A lot of people kept looking back at me and whispering to their friends. It was getting pretty annoying I won't lie.

About thirty minutes go by, and everyone is working. Well, they are supposed to be working at least, many of them are just talking or using their phones.

I was handed a sheet but this was very different from what we were doing at my old school. I did not understand a single thing I saw on my page.

"Aliyia and Zayden can I see you guys for a moment" Ms. Hale announced.

My heart started racing a little bit. More stares came my way as I walked to her desk, meeting up with Zayden once again.

"Aliyia since you are behind on what we have been learning, I'm going to assign Zayden as your tutor to help you prepare for this unit and you have to take the test every student took at the beginning of the school year." She says flipping through papers.

"Oh um okay," I say gripping onto the hem of my shirt once again.

"Zayden are you willing to help her out? This could lead to extra credit" she turns and asks Zayden.

"Nah I don't mind if she's okay with it, although it could be delayed sometimes due to my hockey practices and games."

Ms. Hale nods and sends us back to our seats.

I don't know how I feel about getting tutored by this guy. I'll allow it because he's hot though.

04 | New Friend

Zayden

Aliyia looked so unreal. It shocked me how someone could be so gorgeous.

I could easily tell she has social anxiety so I try not to make her too uncomfortable.

I wanted to sit next to her in math but I knew she would probably get all nervous around me.

I did notice all the people staring and judging her. I even overheard a conversation about her.

One of the girls was saying how the nervousness didn't suit her. The other was judging her outfit and saying she wasn't showing enough skin.

I don't understand how people are so quick to judge a person they do not know. Well in some cases.

❤❤❤❤Aliyia

Math was finally over. I couldn't stand another minute of those girls desperately arching their backs trying to make their asses bigger so boys could notice them.

I thank Ms. Hale as I'm walking out the door and start looking for my next class.

While I'm walking I make eye contact with one of the girls who kept judging me from head to toe.

I try avoiding her but the stuck-up opens her damn mouth.

"Hey you, new girl!" She calls out.

I turn and face her and see her and her friends with their judgemental eyes scanning me.

"We're gonna need you to back off," she says.

Now they are desperately trying to start shit because I just got here and they're telling me to back off from God knows what.

"I don't know what you're talking about" I shrug.

Like I'm not even kidding, I seriously don't know what these attention seekers are looking to gain right now.

"You know very well you were hitting on Zayden in class."

Yup, saying shit for no reason.

"Um, I wasn't? I'm sorry where did you get that from" I say trying to have an attitude but trying to sound genuine at the same time.

"When Ms. Hale called you two up, you got way too close to him for my liking. And you two walked into class together, could it be any more obvious?" She crosses her arms.

Yes, it's official, I am going to kill myself on the first day of school.

"Listen, I don't know who you are or what your business is with him but let me tell you something, I have nothing to do with him and I don't need your judgmental ass going around and talking shit. Please keep your mouth closed and keep my name out of your mouth. I want nothing to do with you at all, I'm just trying to pass my first day of school and you are really pissing me off." I let it out.

All she could do was scoff and give me that annoying look again.

Not wanting to deal with her any longer I walk past the people who came in and watched and make my way to my next class. Oh great, I'm gonna be known as the girl who talked back to the popular girl."

I sat down at the very back of my English class. A few moments later a brunette girl came and sat beside me. She was really beautiful.

She had long beautiful brown hair, green eyes that shined bright, and just perfect features.

"Oh my gosh new girl I just want to say I saw what you said to Kayla and I immediately fell in love with you. Nobody ever puts her or her little crew in their places and them seeing you do that really struck them because it rarely happens. Anyways I'm Tate and I want to be your best fucking friend."

That was a lot of words. It almost flew past my head but I managed to understand it.

"Wow, I'm Aliyia" I greet her.

"Okay, that is the best fucking name I've ever heard. That's it we are officially best friends now" she says playing with one of the rings on her finger.

Never thought I'd make a friend like that but I'll take it. Oh sorry I mean 'Best friend'

I catch myself laughing a little bit as she started engaging in a conversation with me. It felt nice to genuinely speak to someone new who isn't my family, or those mean girls, or Zayden.

Tate seemed like the type to be quite rude to strangers but she was a genuinely nice person.

I explained to her about my moving situation and other things in my life, forgetting to pay attention in class.

"And that'll be your homework for today's class" the teacher announces and dismisses us.

Tate and I just look at each other and immediately start laughing. We were too engaged in a conversation to pay attention in class.

Tate was surely an extrovert so I'm hoping she could just ask someone what we had to do in that class. Soon we were off to different classes and were separated.

My first official friend in the city.

05 | Tutor

A liyia

The day surprisingly flew by quickly and before I knew it the school day was over. I ended up avoiding Kayla and her group the entire day. Luckily I only have one class with them which happens to be math.

During lunch, I ended up meeting Zayden in the cafeteria and he asked if he was able to tutor me after his hockey practice. I agreed and asked for a location and he recommended my house.

I was very hesitant about it but I agreed and he asked me to come watch his hockey practice, then he could drive us both back to my house.

I said I'd think about it because one I barely know the guy, two just no.

I ended up discussing it with Tate and she agreed to come watch the practice with me since her boyfriend was on the team anyways.

School is over so Tate is leading me to the hockey rink. The school is way too big for this, and they somehow fit a literal hockey rink in it.

Kayla just happened to be there. After I spent the entire day avoiding her, I saw her sitting near the rink. She's with her little crew again.

I learned their names throughout the day.

Kayla, Edan, and Trisha.

Kayla gives me a death stare as Tate and I sit near the rink.

Tate just says to ignore her and focus on the practice. It was honestly so boring.

The practice continued for another hour before it was finally over. I dreaded that so much.

Tate met up with her boyfriend and waved goodbye to me as I stayed seated waiting on Zayden.

I started to play with my fingers again. It was a habit, plus I was about to get in a car with a person I barely know.

He seems somewhat genuine but me talking to him for like five minutes doesn't count.

Unlike Tate, we spent the entire day talking to each other so I could say I trust her a little. Although I'm not a trustworthy person.

Minutes later Zayden finally appears on my rear side. "Hey, Aliyia," he says, taking a seat beside me.

"Hi" I mumble.

"Do you have all the books we need?" He asks, trying up the laces of his white converse.

I simply nod.

I follow him out of the school into his car, he sets up a GPS and drives to my new home.

Remembering I don't have a bed or couch we can work on I start bouncing my leg up and down. I felt really nervous and I felt he would judge me.

Even though it's not my fault our furniture is coming later than expected, I just felt the need to explain to him.

But I can't find the words.

He for sure took notice something was wrong due to my facial expression and my leg.

"Hey is everything okay? I'm sorry am I making you nervous?" he asks genuinely.

"No, it's just um" I struggle to find the words. "Since we just moved in, our furniture is coming late so I don't have a bed or couch we can work on." I exhale.

His expression stayed the same like it didn't matter to him.

"Oh don't worry, I don't mind," he says with a smile.

That sorta set my nervousness down. Although I still felt nervous because I'm bringing someone into my home.

I don't know why we couldn't have just worked in the library or something.

I just know after he leaves my mom's gonna ask all sorts of questions. She's always wanted me to have a boyfriend for whatever reason. Sometimes it can get annoying how she taunts me whenever a boy comes over.

We pull up to my house and I unlock the door to find nobody home. Thank the heavens.

"You have a really nice home," he says taking off his shoes.

"Thanks," I say awkwardly.

Oh my goodness I'm so fucking awkward, I wonder how he hasn't ditched me already.

He's been tutoring me for almost two hours now. We are currently studying for the test I have to take at the end of the week. After that, he'll begin teaching me the current unit.

I've learned a little more about him over the past two hours.

Actually, the first ten minutes were spent with him talking about his life and everything.

According to his words, he's been playing hockey since he was six years old. He's always wanted to play professional hockey in the NHL ever since he learned about hockey.

"Would you like a snack or something?" I ask standing up from the floor.

He lifts his head from the textbook and looks me straight in the eye. "No thank you" he kindly says, turning his attention back to the textbook.

I grab myself a glass of ice-cold water as I make my way back to our studying area.

Another hour of studying before he finally closes up his textbook.

"Sorry I have to start going now" he puts his textbook in his bag. "How about you work on these questions and we can work on it together tomorrow, alright?" he speaks, pointing to the questions in my textbook.

"Mhm," I hum.

When he's leaves I let out a groan I've been wanting to let out. No way a student just assigned me homework.

It was almost 9 pm, and for the first time in a while, I felt like sleeping early.

I leave the living room floor after packing up all the materials I used for my tutoring session and go straight to my room.

After I got changed, I crashed into my blankets and fell victim to sleep.

06 | Bed Box

A liyia

Another school day. Another day of having to see Kayla and her puppets. Another day of seeing Zayden, meaning another day of studying.

My bedding stuff arrives today but it arrives when nobody but me is home. Well, Zayden will be here for my tutoring session.

Getting up from bed, I take a nice hot shower and pick out the first set of clothes I see. It happens to be a plain black cami top and grey sweatpants.

I pair that up with white Nike Air Force 1s and silver jewelry.

Aurora drives me to school again and we engage in some small talk on the way. We are talking about how our first days went and Aurora is rambling about some cute guys she saw there.

Aurora is an extrovert. She could talk to anyone, and she could yell at anyone or anything that pisses her off.

When she drops me off and drives away, I start receiving looks from people. Some were looks of disgust, some were looks of joy, and some were looks of "oh my gosh she's hot". I could tell a lot by facial expressions.

I'm a reader. I can read people like I can read pages of a book.

The first period made me want to kill myself. One, Tate isn't in that class. Two, Kayla and her puppets are in this class and keep looking back at me. Three, It's literally math. Who enjoys math? Especially at eight o clock in the morning.

Twenty minutes into class, someone rushed into the classroom in the middle of the lesson.

Zayden.

He had morning hair, making him look like he just woke up and he was panting like crazy.

"Sorry I'm late, I woke up late" he apologizes to the teacher.

As he makes his way to sit somewhere, he locks eyes with me and changes his course of direction my way. I silently pray that he isn't going to sit beside me, and my prayers failed.

He came and sat right next to me, scooting his chair a little closer.

"Hey, Ali," he says, leaning on the table.

"Hi," I mumble.

"Did you finish the math questions I asked you to work on?" He asks, taking out his textbook to follow along.

"Yeah, I-" I was cut off by a mention of my name.

"Aliyia and Zayden, you two have something you would like to share with the class?" Ms hale calls us out.

All eyes turned to us and I shrank when I saw the number of snickers coming from around the room. Unknowingly my leg started to bounce up and down, from all the looks I was getting.

I couldn't speak, I heard my gulp of fear.

"No ma'am, I'm sorry I was asking her what page we are on in the textbook" A voice from beside me states.

I'm glad he spoke. If I even tried saying a word I would stutter badly and lose all my words in a millisecond.

My leg was bouncing because some people just wouldn't turn their heads away.

Seconds later I felt a hand on my knee. Zayden gives me a reassuring smile as he rubs his thumb over my knee.

That calmed me down just a little bit.

The day went by quickly, thankfully. I met up with Tate during the second period and told her about what happened with Ms. Hale.

Tate and I are currently watching the hockey practice, both waiting for our rides.

"He likes you," Tate says sluggishly grinning.

"What? I've only known him for a day" I lean back in my chair.

"So what?" She shrugs.

"That's weird" I groan.

"Well he has definitely taken an interest in you"

I roll my eyes as she continues babbling on possibilities that he could like me.

Zayden and I are back at my place in the same place we were studying yesterday.

Suddenly there's a ring of a doorbell. I stand up to get it, and Zayden follows behind me.

There's a big box with all the materials needed to set up the box spring. My mattress was also left at the door.

"May I help you with that?" Zayden asks, pointing at the box.

"Yeah, I would appreciate that" I nod.

He helps lift the box into my room then he lifts the mattress and places it outside of my room.

I've already opened the box and looked at the instructions.

Basically, you need to screw each part together or something. My face clearly shows that I'm confused, because of the unclear instructions.

Zayden grabs the instructions from my hand and then asks for a toolbox. I grab the toolbox from the storage room and hand it to him.

He builds it like it's nothing hard.

Thirty minutes into the building he placed the mattress on top. No way that took him only thirty minutes. If I did it alone then I would be stuck until my parents got home just trying to read the instructions.

"Thank you" I face him.

"No problem, Ali." he runs his hands through his hair.

We go back to studying and engage in a little conversation after.

"You've got a good personality, Ali," he says closing his textbook and putting it in his bag.

"What's with the Ali nickname?" I ask, genuinely questioning where it came from.

It sounded familiar from somewhere but I just can't remember where.

"I don't know. It just fits your name I guess. I mean your name is really cute and unique so why not?" He goes on.

My eyes avert from Zayden to the floor.

Wow. I never really thought of my name as 'unique' Although I haven't met someone with my exact name, I know it's not as unique because people have the same name just different spelling I'm guessing.

But him calling my name cute just boosted my confidence a little. I'm not sure why but I felt a spark of confidence run through my body as he said that.

I avert my eyes back to him and clear my throat. "I like your name too, I don't think I've met anyone with that name before"

The light in his eyes dimmed as his face lost a little of the smile.

"Any plans for tomorrow?" he asks, sitting up.

"Nothing, you?"

"I have a hockey game, you should come to watch" he gulps a little.

After I said I didn't know anyone with the name Zayden his expression changed. He looked a little sad at my answer? Not that I'm an expert and reading people even though I said I was. I guess in some ways I'm good at reading people.

"Yeah sure, I'll uh come," I mumble quietly but loud enough for him to hear.

His smile returns as he shoots me a wide grin.

07 | Hockey Game

Zayden

I haven't seen Ali smile yet. I was hoping when I asked her to come to my hockey game she would smile.

All I want right now is just to see her smile.

The first day I went to her house for a tutor session I noticed a picture of a little brunette girl. She looked so familiar to the brunette girl from my childhood.

When I got home that day I found a picture of me and that same exact brunette girl. And that's when I realized who she was.

That's why my expression dimmed when she said she's never met a Zayden before because the Zayden from her childhood was sitting right in front of her.

My hockey team and I are currently having a practice game with each other. The other team arrives in thirty minutes so our game starts soon.

Ali and Tate are already on the benches. They're engaging in a conversation that seems interesting but Ali's still not smiling.

Ali looks my way and catches me staring at her. She tilts her head and furrows her eyebrows a little bit.

"Hey, Zayden snap out of it" a hand waves in my face.

It's my best friend, Lukas. He looks the way I was looking and smirks at me.

"New girl, huh?"

"Bro, stop" I slap his side and stand up from the bench.

He chuckled from behind me and got on the ice for our practice.

❤❤❤❤Aliyia

The hockey game started thirty-five minutes ago. Our school is currently winning. Zayden has made about three goals on his own so far.

I didn't think he was that good. He's really working his ass off though I can tell.

He's made a few glances at me before and during the game, making me wonder what that's all about.

Actually, I've seen him looking at me a lot. Maybe he's judging me. I hope that's not the case.

As Zayden goes for another goal he whips his head over to me and Tate, throws a wink our way then shoots the final goal of the game.

Everyone from our school was cheering loudly, practically screaming at this point.

The hockey team was surrounding Zayden, cheering him on as well.

Tate told me that after a school wins a game, people from that school are allowed to go on the rink and cheer them on from up close so that's exactly what we did along with other people from our school.

My arm was locked with Tate's arm, as we walked onto the ice being very careful not to slip.

Tate slipped away for a moment to go congratulate her boyfriend leaving me on the ice alone. I started carefully walking back to the bleachers not wanting to wait on the ice anymore. As I sat on the bleachers I saw everyone crowded in one area.

Practically everyone is crowding Zayden because he shot the scoring goal, but his eyes are searching for something else, or someone else.

My head drops down to the ground and I stare at my red converse. Just as I was about to stand up and leave I feel a light wind brush past me as someone sits down beside me. "Hey," the voice says.

Zayden.

"Hi, congratulations" I admire his eyes for a moment. They are incredibly gorgeous. I could stare at it all day.

"Thank you, Ali" he sighs.

"Is something wrong? You just scored the winning goal how come you don't seem happy?" I ask concerned.

"No nothing is wrong. I'm just upset I haven't seen you smile yet" he confesses.

I got really taken back by this. He's concerned that he hasn't seen me smile yet. It's not like he should waste his time worrying about that.

"You shouldn't be worried about seeing me smile, focus on your goal. Anyways look I can smile" I shoot him a fake smile.

"But I want to see your real smile. I promise you, I'll make you smile one of these days" he frowns, studying my expression.

Oh.

08 | Cigarettes After Sex

Zayden

Thursday and Friday flew by quickly. On both days I had studying sessions with Ali. Still haven't seen her smile.

Since we won that last game, we have a lot of free time on our hands. Our coach is letting us rest easy for two days.

It's currently Saturday and I'm sitting on my couch watching a marvel movie for the third time in a row today.

As much as I try to stray away from her, my mind just won't stop thinking about her. My mind is eager to see her smile.

Preferably one of the smiles from our childhood. Those were the cutest smiles I'd ever seen.

I have to see her.

I whip out my phone and began texting her contact, asking her if she was busy.

Not long after I get a response from her. "No, I'm free, why?" Was her response.

"Want to try out a diner? It's nearby and it would be a great experience for you to try it out" I text back quickly, eager for her answer.

My finger starts tapping on my knee without me realizing it. It takes her a moment to answer, but her chat bubble finally appears.

"sure what time?" was her response.

We chatted back and forth for a bit, discussing how to get there and what time and we settled on me picking her up at 5:30

At 5:25 I'm already at her house and parked at the side. I messaged her letting her know I'm outside and that she could come whenever she was ready.

Exactly five minutes later, she appears at her door away and looks like she's locking the door. I turn my attention to my phone lock screen to pretend like I didn't see her leave her house.

Ali comes up to the passenger window and knocks on it.

Once she settles in the car, I begin driving to the diner. "Do you want to play music?" I ask her, unlocking my phone.

Don't use your phone and drive!

"Sure, but what if you don't like my music?" she mumbles just loud enough for me to hear.

"It's fine, play whatever you want it's all yours" I reassure her.

She grabs the phone from my hand and begins to type through my Apple Music. The song apocalypse by cigarettes after sex starts to play. Fuck I love this song.

I felt an urge to just sing so that's exactly what I did. "You leapt from crumbling bridges Watching cityscapes turn to dust."

Ali shifts her head to face me and I can see her expression change. She must've been shocked that I know this song, or that I'm singing along to it.

My lips curved up into a smile as I began to sing the next lyrics. "Filming helicopters crashing In the ocean from way above"

"Got the music in you, baby Tell me why" Ali began to sing.

Her voice was very angelic. She sounded like a famous musician but way better. The sound of her singing kept replaying in my head as she continued with the rest of the lyrics.

Somehow, Ali struck him with her voice. Focus on the road he thought almost drifting away from the driving.

We continued to sing the lyrics as we pulled up at the diner. Hearing her angelic voice made me feel things. It was just so perfect, I just want to hear it again.

As we sat in the diner enjoying the warm food placed in front of us, my mind went straight to the moment in the car when she started singing. I want to know more about if she wants to sing in the future because she definitely should. She has the voice of an angel. Not just singing, her voice is just angelic in general.

"Have you ever thought of being a singer?" I ask her, dipping my fry in my milkshake and plopping it in my mouth.

She nods, forcing a smile. "Yeah, it's my dream"

The smile on my face slightly faded when I realized she used a fake smile. Planting the smile back on my face, I respond.

"You should be a singer or musician, your voice is angelic and perfect," I say, studying her expression.

"Should I?" she repositions herself in her seat.

"Yeah, I'd be your first fan and your number one fan" I joke with a little bit of seriousness in my tone. I wasn't exactly lying. If she did become a singer or anything I would undyingly be her number one fan.

Suddenly, the thing I'd been waiting for appeared. Ali's gaze softened and a smile worked its way up to touch the corners of her mouth.

A real smile.

I held a huge smile on my face as my eyes twinkled. I was relieved. I finally got to see her real smile. Ali had dimples too, I didn't think it was possible for a person to get more cuter than they already are.

This is a smile I had to absorb quickly because just as it came it disappeared in the blink of an eye. Her smile disappearing didn't make me drop my smile. Instead, I kept the same smile.

It was a smile of joy, satisfaction, and relief.

"You finally learned to smile again" I let out, my gaze never drifting from her.

"Again?" she questions, taking a sip of her chocolate milkshake.

"Never mind" I mumble, keeping the same pleased smile planted on my face.

Finally.

❤❤❤❤Authors Note

OMG SHE FINALLY SMILED

Ugh I love them so much and I just want them to kiss but I want this to be a slow burn but I'm also way too impatient for that

Let me know things to add to make this better

A somewhat cute chapter for u guys

09 | Letters

Z ayden

Last night I got to see her smile. Her real smile. I could tell it was a genuine smile so that explains why I acted as I did. Sorta. Honestly, I'm just fascinated by her in general.

The fact that she was my childhood best friend made me more interested in her. Although her not remembering who I am does make me sad. I'm just hoping she remembers who I am and just doesn't recognize it's me.

Because we made a promise when I moved that no matter what we would never forget each other. I kept my promise so I hope she did too.

A pounding knock on my bedroom door appears. For fucks sake.

I ignore the knock and a few seconds later, the same pounding knock bangs on my door.

"Fuck off, Summer!" I yell at her through the closed doors.

I knew it was summer because both our parents were at work right now. If it was my mother consider me dead because she would not handle that disrespect. I would get the slap of my life if I spoke to her light that.

"Zayden open the door!" Summer yelled continuing to bang on my door.

Children.

Forcing myself to get up, I unlock my door and stare at my sister who holds a box in her hand.

"What do you want" I roll my eyes at her.

"I found this box of memories with you and your old friends, I thought you might want it," she says holding out the box for me to grab.

She's doing something nice for me. For once. She's not all sweet as she sounds. She's vicious.

Summer is literally demonic. The other day she started pretending like her bones were cracking as a reference to Stranger Things.

Taking the box from her hand, I thank her and shut the door, locking it.

I sit on my bed and begin to open the box. It's filled with pictures, papers, and bracelets.

I randomly grab something and the first thing I grab was two matching bracelets.

Somehow, I remember the origin of these bracelets. Childhood me and childhood Aliyia begged our parents to buy us separate matching bracelets.

One was to use for the both of us together and the other was for our future relationships. We were weird 8-year-olds.

I smile at the memory, placing the object to the side. The next thing I grabbed was a picture.

I also remember this. It was taken on one of those cameras Aliyia got for Christmas. It's a picture of us sitting near a river. That river used to be our favorite spot.

And also the tree beside the river. We begged our parents to let us go there together all the time. Best times.

I look through all the photos of us as children and smile at them. She's changed quite a bit.

She was a natural brunette as a kid. But guess she dyed her hair blonde.

Honestly brunette was the best but that doesn't make her any less beautiful to me.

Setting the picture down, I reach for the last few papers in the box. Notes and letters.

Notes we snuck to each other during class and letters we often wrote when we were bored.

I read the first note and cringed at my writing and spelling.

I am hungre I want lunch alreade I hate math so much what did you mom pack for lunch? My mama packed me chickan and rice :)

-zay zay

Zay Zay. I remember that nickname. I think Aliyia made that up because apparently saying my full name was boring to her.

Picking up another note, I smile. Aliyias's writing as a kid was amazing, even to this day. Guess it's just a natural talent of hers.

Karter is so mean to me. He keeps yelling at me for messing up :(I just want him to move schools. I cant stand him.. also I have a sandwhich for lunch and a juice box

-Liyia

She spelled 'sandwich' wrong but that makes it funnier. I want her to realize who I am, maybe I could get my best friend back.

10 | Snowman

A liyia

    I've been in New York for almost three weeks now.

Tate and I have gotten a lot closer, along with Zayden and I. Tate introduced me to her boyfriend Lukas and I found out that Zayden and Lukas are best friends.

The four of us have kinda became a friend group. We hang out a lot at school and they always make Tate and I come to their practices and games.

I've already completed the test my teacher arranged for me to take. Now Zayden and I mainly just have daily study sessions.

I like to call them studying sessions instead of tutoring even though half the time we study together he ends up teaching me and helping me.

He for real teachers me for than the math teacher does. That says a lot, doesn't it?

The snow started to fall this morning and it's gotten colder out.

My outfit of the day was just a plain blue sweatshirt and khaki cargo pants, along with white Air Force 1s.

Basic but at least it looked good on me.

I'm currently walking side by side with Tate on our way to our P.E class. One of the worst classes, after math of course.

Zayden and Lukas are also in this class meaning it wouldn't just be the two of us. One negative thing about it is Tate always clings to her boyfriend, making me feel more single than ever.

I've never had my first kiss yet, I haven't even had a boyfriend. Sad right.

As school ended, the snow had risen. A lot more than this morning.

The group was walking out and into Zaydens car. "We should make a snowman" Tate suggests, nuzzling against her boyfriend.

"The snow isn't sticky, dumbass" Zayden says, putting the car in reverse and pulling out of the student parking lot.

"Water" I blurt.

"That won't make it sticky" Lukas questions.

"Yes it will," Tate says slapping his thigh.

"I guess we'll have to find out." Zayden shrugs.

It worked. We poured some water onto the fresh snow and it became slightly sticky. Sticky enough to build something at least.

And just like that, the assembling of the snowman began. Tate was preparing snow for us by luring the water all over.

Lukas was rolling up the stomach and Zayden was rolling up a big snowball.

And I was just rolling the head because I had no energy to make a big snowball or anything like that. Too much effort for me.

And just like that, the snowman was established. The last final touches needed were the sticks, rocks, carrots, and a hat.

Cliche snowman but honestly who cares.

Tate and I helped add the finishing touches. With that, our cliche snowman was complete. "What should we name it?" I ask, scanning our work from head to its imaginary toes.

"let's name her crystal," Tate says, smiling excitedly.

"That sounds good" Zayden adds, standing close tome.

"Well.." Lukas begins but stops when he sees Tate glaring at him. "It's amazing" he laughs it off awkwardly.

We admire our snowman together, taking pictures, and having a conversation with it. Yes, a conversation with a snowman, what's wrong with that?

I guess I could say I love my new friends. Their humor is incredible, they are kind, and overall just great people.

In some ways I guess I could say I'm glad we moved here. Some ways.

11 | Skating

A liyia

A week has passed by since we built our snowman, or should I say snowwoman. It still stands to this day in my front yard.

Parts of it are covered in extra snow that fell recently.

The group and I have gotten way closer within these last few weeks. Almost inseparable. Tate is the best person here.

She was the first person to welcome me to New York so I have a special place for her in my heart. And I guess Zayden too, although I've known and been closer to Tate for a longer amount of time.

I'm currently sitting in my art classroom, doodling a picture of a marvel character. I love marvel.

A knock on the classroom door filled the silence of the classroom.

Most people shot their heads at the door, waiting for the teacher to open it.

When the teacher opened the classroom door, a very tall tan man stood stiff with a bouquet of flowers in his hand. "I have flowers for" the man started to speak, pausing to read the note. "Aliyia Grace?"

What the hell.

Practically everyone turned to look my way. Some smirking, some with looks of jealousy, and some expressionless faces.

"That's me" I raised my hand.

The man made his way over to me after the teacher let him in, putting the flowers in my hand. "Who are these from?" I ask, looking at the card.

"I'm not sure, I was just told to deliver these flowers to you," he says, putting his hand in his pocket. His face was expressionless.

Who would send me flowers, and why?

"Oh, thank you" I smile, setting the flowers down on the table.

He nods and makes his way for the exit of the classroom. It killed me that Tate wasn't in this class with me. Attention was all I was getting right now. People kept looking back at me and whispering.

Like oh my gosh, just do your damn work man.

Good thing school flew by fast because I couldn't handle any more looks from all the jealous people.

Tate was so happy when she found out someone sent me flowers. For whatever reason she was jumping up and down, squealing.

I am curious myself on who sent me them, I want to thank them but I also want to ask them why they gave it to me out of all people.

Tate and I sat at the hockey rink bleachers. Zayden and Lukas had another practice today. The team's next upcoming game is next week so they've got a lot of extra practice.

Just like every other practice, Zayden would always take glances at me at any opportunity. I don't get it, he does that at every practice I come to.

Maybe he just likes looking at my face, honestly me too. Who wouldn't want to look at my face?

After practice, Tate embraced me in a hug before leaving with her boyfriend, Lukas. Apparently, they had a special date planned.

I want a love like theirs one day. My day will come, hopefully.

I noticed Zayden was still in the rink, circling it.

Standing from my seat, I make my way onto the rink being careful with each step. "What are you doing?" I ask, almost catching up with him.

"What does it look like? I'm skating." His response was sassy. Whore.

"But practice is over," I say, catching myself from slipping.

"And"

"Stop sassing me"

"I'm not"

"Yes you are"

"No, I'm not"

"You are"

"Not"

"Are"

"Shut up"

I smirk to myself knowing I won that. "I win," I say smiling right in his face. We always have 'arguments' like that and I always end up winning because he's whipped.

"This time," Zayden says rolling his eyes.

"All the time"

His eyes searched around, the rink before he started skating toward me.

With fear, I tried running away but I ended up slipping on the ice while doing so.

Luckily I was caught, right before smashing my face on the ice. Zayden used one had to hold my waist and the other to hold my arm.

"Screw you" I grip onto his hockey shirt.

Zayden started to laugh softly, his eyes mocking me. "You're fault"

"It's cause you started chasing me causing me to run, it's a natural response," I say, crossing my arms and facing the ice.

"Do you know how to skate?" He asks, a smile creeping onto his face.

"No, why?" I question, letting go of his shirt.

"I'll teach you, we have some spare skates I can give you to practice with"

"Why should I?"

"Because you suck at balancing with just your shoes, imagine using skates." His tone was confident.

Bitch.

"Fuck you"

"And also the school provides a trip to a skating rink every year so if you don't know to skate you're going to look like a fool." He says straight out, no hesitation in his voice.

"Fine, you're a bitch by the way" I admit, letting him guide me to where the shoes are.

He just shoots me that damn teasing smile again.

I'll severely hurt this guy if he kills me, ill make him cry and make him go to heaven and back.

12 | Hot Chocolate

Zayden

"Don't make me fall!" Ali whines, gripping onto me so tight, that I'll probably see a mark later.

"I won't relax, you can stop gripping onto me so hard," I say, holding her hand and helping her walk on the ice.

"I swear if you-" she begins but I stop her before she can finish.

"Shh, just trust me"

Ali just rolls her eyes at me and grips my shoulder even tighter.

Minutes later she starts getting the hang of it and next thing you know she's taking huge steps on the ice.

"Great, I can teach you how to actually skate now," I say, eager to watch her skate without harshly gripping onto me.

"Who needs to know how to skate when you can just walk on the ice?" She replies sarcastically.

I step behind her and grab a hold of her waist.

"Alright Ali, just push forward off one leg and let the other glide through the ice" I instruct.

She tries to follow my instructions but causes us both to stumble and land butt first on the ice. "Oops," she says innocently, trying not to laugh.

A smile worked it's way up her face as she tried her hardest not to laugh. Whenever she smiles my body just naturally reacts and brings up its own smile.

Whenever she's not around, a lot of my smiles are forced. Sometimes at least.

Most of my smiles now are directed to her, and my mother. I guess Lukas and Tate too. That's it mainly though.

"Let's try again" I set my gaze onto her eager face. "Just watch me and look at my feet, not in a weird way though" I chuckled.

Ali shot me a seductive fake wink and started to focus on my feet as I glided through the ice.

Her beauty was so much for me to handle. Ali is the girl of my dreams. She's just too beautiful to be real. She's much more beautiful than models you see on television, and don't get me wrong they are beautiful too but Ali is just something else.

Thoughts of Ali surrounded my head, causing me to get distracted and slam right into the board of the rink.

Well, that fucking hurt.

Ali's eyes widened as she let out the loudest laugh I'd ever heard from her. She didn't even attempt to help me or anything, she just sat on the ice, laughing at me.

"Do you find that amusing?" I ask her, stabilizing myself.

"Very much, yes," she says in between laughs. "You have to focus, Zayden" a little bit of mocking in her voice.

"I am focused." I roll my eyes.

"No, you aren't"

"Don't start that again, Ali."

She gets up on her feet and starts practicing with me again.

Our little skating lesson lasted an hour before we both started getting tired of it. During most of the lesson, Ali just started bursting out laughing out of nowhere then says it's cause of me slamming right into the board.

She just won't let it go.

"I want hot chocolate," Ali says, taking off her skates and placing them in the bucket where they came from.

"We can go to my house, you haven't been there anyways" I suggest, putting a few things in my hockey bag.

Ali agrees and soon we're headed out of the school hockey rink.

The drive to my house was filled with screaming Taylor Swift lyrics and Ali mocking me by slamming into the car window.

She even made a visual representation of what I looked like, in the car.

"It's not that funny," I say annoyed, pulling into my driveway.

"But it really is, you should've seen your face" she laughs with this adorable laugh.

My mom is home, her car is parked neatly in the driveway. I swear if she asks all types of questions to Ali, I am going to lose my shit. Not at her, if I did she would have no hesitation slapping the sense out of me.

Unlocking the door with my house key, I let Ali enter first then follow in once she's made room for me to enter, closing the door behind me.

"Mama? I'm home!" I shout, letting her know I'm home.

It's a daily routine.

I walk into the kitchen, Ali sitting on the chair in the kitchen island, and pull out a container of hot chocolate.

I heat the milk and place the hot chocolate powder in it afterward. "Marshmallows?" I ask, taking hot the bag of mini marshmallows.

"Yes please," Ali replies, her eyes looking around my house.

Seconds later, I hand Ali her hot chocolate and lead her upstairs. Just as I thought we were gonna get away with avoiding my mom, her bedroom door shoots open and my mother comes out of it, smiling at me.

"Zay Zay, how was practice? You're a little later today, I thought you didn't have tutoring?" My mother says, embracing me in a hug.

Before I can respond to her, she already has another thing to say. "Oh, and who's this beautiful lady? Is she the one who you tutor?"

"Yes, she is the one I tutor mom. And I'm late because I was helping her learn to skate."

"Oh, that's sweet. Well, you two have fun, maybe not too much fun but enjoy your hot chocolates" My mom says, rushing down the stairs. Probably to catch the next episode of The Real Housewives.

"Mom!" I groan and scrunch my face up in disgust. Ali just stood there with a wide smile, even after my mom was gone.

I led her into my room and sat on the chair, while she sat on the bed.

"Your mom is nice," Ali says, sipping her hot chocolate.

"Most days, yeah" I admit. "Want to watch a movie?" I ask, flipping the remote up in the air.

"Sure"

"You pick." I point the remote to her.

"No, you"

"No, I say you pick."

"It's your house"

"You're the guest"

"So what? It's your house, you pick the movie"

"No"

"Yes"

"Yes," I pause when I realize what I said. "Wait no!" I say hurriedly.

"Hah too late, I win again!"

"Fuck you" I groan, starting to search for a movie "I'll win one of these days, just wait and see"

Ali just hums a sarcastic hum and waits for me to pick a movie.

The effect this girl has on me.

13 | Waffles

Aliyia

I woke up to vigorous knocking on my door. Except it wasn't my door, not even my bedroom. It was quite larger and less decorated.

I was sleeping on a large king bed, and a giant figure was passed out next to me.

Zayden was drooling in his sleep. He was facing me with one hand under his pillow and the other laid on my waist. Weird.

It took me one whole long minute to process everything that happened yesterday. We had hot chocolate, binged a few movies, then I assume we both passed out in the process.

The knock on the door became louder and more aggressive. Zayden didn't look like he was gonna wake up from an aggressive knock, so I gently stood up trying not to wake him up from his peaceful sleep.

Tiptoeing to the door, I open it and see a younger girl who was about one inch shorter than me. She gave me a confused look, probably wondering who I am.

"Who are you?" She questions, trying to look past the door to see a still passed-out Zayden. "Are you his girlfriend?" She asked, a little excitement in her voice.

"No no I'm Zaydens friend, I accidentally fell asleep here last night" I responded a little awkwardly. All I received was a mouthed "oh" from her.

"I'm Summer, his little sister" she introduces herself and pauses waiting for me to introduce myself.

"I'm Aliyia, Zayden calls me Ali so you can too if you want"

"Well nice to meet you, Ali. Tell Zayden when he wakes up that he promised to drive me to the mall with my friends today"

"Okay, see you later Summer" I wave her off and shut the door, locking it.

I lay back down on the bed, facing away from Zayden on my phone. Somehow, a warm hand snuck its way onto my waist, holding it for their dear life.

"Zayden" I whisper feeling him shift closer, hand still on my waist.

"Ali" he groans.

"Wake up" I demand, getting another groan from him as he nuzzles his head in the back of my neck.

"Five more minutes" he lets out, holding onto my waist tighter.

"Five more minutes." I smile, returning to my phone.

Exactly five minutes later I force Zayden out of his bed receiving groans and moans while doing so. He's finally sat up in his bed, eyes half-closed.

"Why are you waking me up so early" his morning voice speaks.

His morning voice is quite attractive. Not that low but it's way lower than his regular voice. His regular voice is already low enough.

"Because I wanted to" I give him a teasing smile.

"I don't like when you tease me" he complains, crossing his arms with his sleepy eyes.

"Wake up" I demand again, clapping my hands in his face.

"Fine, fine," he says opening his eyes fully. Good.

"Do you want something to eat?" He asks rising from his bed and heading to his washroom to wash his face.

"Yes, what are the options?"

"Waffles," he says bluntly, walking out of the washroom.

"Anything else?" I question.

"Yes but I want waffles so you're having waffles" he smiles lazily.

"Screw you" I joke, rolling my eyes.

"When?" He winks and smirks.

"No."

We head downstairs to see Summer eating a bowl of cereal while on her phone watching what looks like Stranger Things.

"Hey Ali," Summer greets.

"Hi Summer" I wave, sitting down next to her while Zayden gets the ingredients for waffles. "Just make eggos," I tell Zayden. Way simpler, quicker, and fills your hunger. Not to mention it's so delicious.

"How do you guys know each other?" He asks continuing to ignore my remark.

"Oh Ali and I go a long way" Summer jokes, placing her hand on my shoulder. She receives a Yeah from me.

"Don't call her that." He demands, an annoyed look on his face.

"What? Ali?" Summer questions, placing her bowl in the sink."

"Yes."

"Why?" Summer asks, washing her dish.

"Because that's my nickname for her" he crosses his arms, waiting for the waffles to be ready.

"Your point?" Summer talks back.

"Don't call her that or you're gonna lose your personal driver"

"Fine" she groans "bitch" she mumbles that last part out, loud enough for only me to hear.

Zayden has a smug grin on his face showing that he's proud of himself for what he did. Bitchy move in my opinion. It's my name I should pick if I want her to call me Ali and I personally don't mind.

"That was mean and unnecessary" I admit, getting up to stand beside him.

"How?" He asks innocently with that same smug grin face on his face.

"It's my name,"

"It's my nickname"

"And? Who said she couldn't call me that?"

"I did"

"Who gave you the right to decide that?"

"Me, I gave myself the right" he glances at the waffles then back at me.

Not even wanting to respond, I roll my eyes and sit back down waiting for my waffles. Two minutes later a stacked plate of waffles swirled with whipped cream and drizzled in chocolate with a cherry on top was placed in front of me.

"So cliché" I laugh.

"It's good" he shrugs sitting beside me.

"Where's yours?" I ask him, seeing he sat beside me with no plate and only a fork.

"What do you mean? We are clearly sharing" he smirks.

He's doing this on purpose.

"Get your own" I slide the plate father from him.

"Hey! There are not enough ingredients for separate plates."

"Fine" I mumble, letting him share with me.

The moment I put the waffle in my mouth I felt like something just exploded in my mouth. It was so damn delicious. I could seriously eat his every day and not complain. Where the hell did he learn to make waffles like this?

"Delicious right?" Zayden asks, taking a piece from my plate.

"It's alright" I mumble. It's not alright, it's way better than alright. Alright is an understatement. It's heavenly.

"Mhm," he hums.

"Hey I forgot to tell you but remember your driving your sister to the mall with her friends"

He lets a loud groan. "Can you come with me? I don't want to be stuck in a car with a bunch of children" he asks.

"Sure why not"

❤❤❤❤Authors Note

THIS CHAP IS RLLY BORING I'M SORRY. ANYWAYS SUMMER GRYANT HAS MADE HER APPEARANCE

14 | Mall

Z ayden

Ali and I went to her house so that she could change into fresh clothes. I sat on her couch as she was upstairs, most likely changing by now.

Aurora, Ali's sister approaches me and engages me in a conversation with her. She started questioning me, asking if I was her boyfriend yet. The first time I met Aurora she attacked me with questions just like now.

She won't let go of the fact that we aren't together. Every time I tell her we aren't she always adds a yet at the end.

I assume she wants us together. I could get with that. Ali came rushing down the stairs, stopping my conversation with her sister.

Ali was wearing black flared leggings, a striped green and blue sweatshirt, and black converse. Her outfits are everything.

"Ready?" I ask tossing my keys in the air, catching them as gravity pushes them down.

Ali nods. "Yeah"

"Alright let's go then," I say, following her out the door.

"Aux?" I ask, putting on my seatbelt and starting up the car. Ali nods and grabs my phone from me. Not long after "finesse" by Bruno Mars starts playing. Ali shoots me a knowingly look, she knows I'm gonna start singing it.

With a playful smile, I start singing the chorus as it comes up.

"When I'm walkin' with you I watch the whole room change Baby, that's what you do No, my baby, don't play Blame it on my confidence Oh, blame it on your measurements Shut that shit down on sight That's right"

I couldn't help myself, that part is just too good. Ali silently judges me while facing the window. I can see her smiling in the window reflection and I can hear her bits of laughter that are trying so hard not to slip out.

"For your information, I am an amazing singer. I'm practically an expert" I smile, trying to keep my own laughter from coming out.

"Uh-huh, sure." Is all I get as she goes back to her silenced judging.

❤❤❤❤Aliyia

Being stuck in a car with children made my brain tickle. They kept hassling us asking if we were together. I didn't even know the kids yet they were so intrigued by my supposed love life with Zayden.

Zayden tried to convince his sister to make her friends stop asking about our "love life" but instead she continued asking questions.

"Have you guys done it yet?" One of them blurts out. Me and Zayden look at each other with the same agape expressions.

"Um, you guys are what? 12? 13? That's a bit too much for you" I finally speak up, considering Zayden did most of the talking.

"And? Who asked you Ms, Fiesty" another one speaks. Lord help me, I am not going to fight with a twelve-year-old right now.

"She was just saying, plus don't speak to her like that or you girls lose your ride." Zayden defends me, speaking in a childish tone probably trying to match theirs.

Summer slaps the girl who talked back to me on her shoulder and gave her an annoyed look. Probably cause of Zayden saying they could probably lose their ride if they spoke to me like that.

It was very cute that he defended me. Still annoyed at that twelve-year-old though. It was disturbing for them to ask that question anyways. What did they expect? For us to tell them if we did or not in full detail? It's not like we did or ever will do.

He's my best friend, nothing else. I think?

❤❤❤❤Zayden

We finally got some peace after dropping the girls at the mall. Instead of leaving right away we stopped by the mall and are currently in Garage. Ali dragged me here just to shop for herself.

I'm currently sitting on one of the dressing room chairs waiting for Ali. She comes out in black cargo pants and a long sleeve-cropped plain blue top.

Ali starts twirling around for me, giving me a full 360 of her outfit. "What do you think? Should I get it?" She asks, a wide grin on her face.

I look at the outfit once more and nod my head in agreement. "You definitely should, it suits you"

Ali squeals and returns to her dressing room, returning in less than five minutes. "Are we good to go?" I ask her as we approach the cashier.

"Yup."

Just as Ali was about to take out her money, I pull out my card and begin to pay. "Dude," Ali says in confusion.

"What are you doing?" Ali asks, crossing her arms.

"What does it look like? I'm paying." I respond sarcastically. I know it annoys her when I'm sarcastic towards her.

"I see that. Why? I was just about to pay"

"Because why not?"

"I don't need you to buy me things, I have money y'know"

"Spend as much as my money as you want" I shrug, taking the bag from the cashier and walking out with it. Ali tries to argue more but I shut her up by agreeing to buy her food from the food court if she accepts that I paid for her.

"We should go swimming" Ali suggests, taking a bite out of her burger.

Shit.

Forgot to mention to her that I cannot swim. Like actually I will fucking drown. The last time I tried swimming it was in the deep end I kid you not, I sank.

"We should"

"Let's go now, I'll text Tate and you text Lukas and we can all go as a group." She speaks excitedly. I just know when I tell her I can't swim she will have no problem laughing in my face.

"Okay."

I'm going to break down if I drown in front of my friends.

15 | Pool

Aliyia

I'm excited to go swimming. I got a new bikini a few weeks ago. Zayden looked a little hesitant when I asked him to go swimming.

We had to make another stop at both our houses to collect our swimming gear, and now we're on our way to pick up Tate and Lukas. Tate is hanging out with Blake so we kinda crashed them but they didn't seem to mind.

Zayden honks the car horn when we pull up to Tate's house. Two seconds later she comes rushing out of her house, Lukas behind her with a bag that she probably made him carry.

"Hi, Lia" Tate greeted as she entered the car, sitting directly behind me.

"Hi, Tate" I greet her back cheerfully.

"What pool are we going to? Lukas asks, buckling up Tate's seatbelt for her, then buckling up his own.

"Not sure of the name but it's in the south," Zayden replies, moving his hands on the steering wheel so majestically.

When my father told me we were moving here I was excited. I should've been excited since I've wanted to live here since I was a kid but the thought of leaving all my "friends" and all the memories I made there made me want to stay.

I wish I listened when adults would say "cherish every moment of your childhood" because now I wish I could relive it.

But now I'm sort of glad we moved here. Not so much but I've made a friend group already, and not to mention this place is just wonderful.

I love it here.

Just the outside of the building was already big, I can't imagine how big it is inside.

Another thing about me is I love swimming. I'm a naturally good swimmer. My parents just threw me in a pool one day and I just picked up the ability ever since.

My thought was correct. It is indeed bigger on the inside. There were many pool sections and each of them was so big.

Tate and I head into the ladies' change room while Lukas and Zayden went into the men's change room. Minutes later we all arrive out of the change rooms at the same moment. Coincidence.

"Ali, come here for a sec" Zayden gestured to me, as we walked away from Tate and Lukas.

"What's up?"

"Well um" he starts. He looks like he can't find the words of what he's going to say next. "I like, can't swim" he whispers.

I stare at him blankly as he returns the same expression to me. I would show remorse but instead, I just burst out laughing in his face. Yes, it's mean, but yes I will continue.

"It's not funny" Zayden pouts.

That's so adorable, he's this sunshine but grumpy guy at school yet he can't swim? My days here keep getting better and better.

"You're right," I say, trying to keep my face blank. "It's hilarious"

"I was never taught, okay?"

"I was never taught either, my parents just threw me in a pool and forced me to swim. Maybe I should do that to you." I laugh.

"I'm a grown man, you can't just throw me in a pool," Zayden says, confidence in his voice.

"Grown man? We might need to work on your terms for yourself, they need to be more accurate"

Zayden flips me off and walks away, returning to Lukas and Tate.

Absolutely hilarious. You would think he would know how to swim based on his looks and personality yet he cannot.

Hope he at least knows how to doggy paddle.

We've been swimming for about twenty minutes now and Zayden remains in the kiddy pool. From what I saw he made friends with a little girl and now they're splashing each other like little kids. Well, it's probably normal for her to splash like a little kid considering she is one, but it's adorable to see Zayden doing it as well.

When Zayden told Tate he couldn't swim, she laughed hard in his face which then rose mylaughter again from the grave.

And ever since he's been sitting in the kiddie pool, looking like
a loner. Maybe I should approach him and comfort him? Such a
whipped thing to do, to be honest, but oh well.

I quickly exit the deep end of the pool and make my way toward
the kiddie pool. Zayden is still playing with that little girl.

"Hey" I speak, entering the cold kiddie pool.

Zayden looks up from the little girl and meets my eyes. His eyes fall
to my hair, then my eyes, then back to my hair, then my eyes again.

"Your hair is brown," he says, letting his eyes fall back to my hair.

"Oh, it just does that every time I swim. It lets me be a brunette for
less than an hour too, isn't that cool?" I chuckle.

"Sucks because I like your blonde hair, but honestly I'd like to see
you with brunette hair." He shrugs, touching my hair. "Anyways this
is Evelyn, my new best friend"

My jaw falls into the deep end. Ouch, calling this pretty little girl
his best friend cuts deeper than a knife. But I play it cool anyways.

"Hi Evelyn I'm Aliyia, Zayden's old best friend"

Evelyn shoots me a wide grin then goes back to splashing Zayden.
As they're splashing each other Zayden points at me and soon they're
both splashing me.

"Oh, it's on" was all that left my mouth before I started splashing
both of them twice as quickly as they did to me.

I stopped splashing for a moment and tried to scan the pool for
Lukas and Tate, only to find them making out in a hot tub. Never
mind.

Never thought in my first weeks of being in New York I would be splashing a little girl and a teenager named Zayden Gryant. I honestly would have laughed in your face if you told me that would be my future. But here it is.

❤❤❤❤Authors Note

I'm thinking of making that little girl Evelyn have at least one or two appearances in the book. Let me know.

Anyways it's finally summer for me (school ended on the 29th) so expect more content, or not bc I might actually have a life this summmer

But my goal for this summer is to finish this book! I might also private my other book because it's really boring and I want to focus on this.

Plus I have a series in mind that I want to write but I'm going to finish this first. So hopefully we can expect the first book of the series I want to write in the fall.

16 | Atlantis

Zayden

Hockey practice was the most annoying thing ever. It usually makes me want to kill myself the way the coach makes us practice. He makes us work hard till we are sweating. That doesn't even sound bad but trust me it's worse.

Winter break was coming up and exams were too. Aliyia and I have been studying a lot more recently, although most of our study sessions are spent screaming Taylor Swift.

It's an addiction.

"Let's make cookies or something I'm tired of this" Aliyia says shutting her textbook.

"But Ali, exams."

"I don't care" she stands up and exits her room.

Might as well follow her instead of just sitting here in her room like a clown.

"So what cookies are we making?" I ask her, helping her take out some ingredients from the fridge.

"Chocolate chip, best kind and easiest to make" she replies, sounding annoyed. She started taking out the chocolate chips, flour, baking soda, and vanilla extract. The way she aggressively grabbed each ingredient showed she was in a bad mood.

I won't push her to talk for now.

She starts pouring all the ingredients into a bowl and gives me the job of mixing it. Curiousness flooded through me and I licked the spoon after finishing mixing.

Oh my goodness, these are the best chocolate chip cookies I've ever tasted and I'm not even joking. Tied with my mom.

The familiar taste of cookies from my childhood brought a smile to my face.

"How is it?" Ali asks, taking the spoon from me and licking it herself. Her face lights up and sudden energy shows up. "Damn, that's fucking good"

I nod in agreement and grab another spoon to eat the cookie dough with.

Unfortunately, we ended up eating basically all the cookie dough leaving only enough for fewer cookies than we'd like.

"Jackass why'd you eat all the cookie dough," Ali says, the annoyed tone returning to her calm expression.

"Hey don't blame me, you ate half of it too" I defend myself.

"Pig" she mumbles.

"I heard that" I cross my arms.

"Good."

Retreating from her for a moment, I rush up the stairs to grab my speaker then rush down the stairs to see Ali putting as many cookies as she can fit onto a cookie sheet.

After, Ali connects to the speaker and starts playing her playlist from Spotify.

Atlantis by Seafret starts playing just as rain begins to hit the ground. Perfect setting.

For some reason, this song fits the scenery outside.

"Will you grant me a dance, m'lady?" I tease, putting my hand out for Ali to grab.

She still shoots me an annoyed glare but takes my hand anyways, showing a slight smile that she is clearly trying to hide.

"I can't dance," Ali says, looking down.

I use my pointer finger to raise her chin so her eyes meet mine.

"Don't worry I don't either, let's improvise" I chuckle, giving her a cheeky grin.

Both my hands meet her waist while both of hers meet each side of my shoulders. Her expression once again changed but this time into a flustered expression.

"Isn't this a slow dancing position?" Ali asks nervously.

"I'm pretty sure it is but oh well" I shrug, trying to sway to the song.

I definitely got way too into it because as I tried being confident with my moves, I stepped on Ali's foot causing her to yelp.

"Shit, sorry" I apologize holding back a laugh.

Ali for sure noticed my expression because she hit my chest and turned away. "It's not funny that hurt jackass"

"Didn't I say I was sorry? What else should I do, kiss your feet" I tease letting the laugh flow out.

Ali thinks like she's considering it for a moment. "Actually, yes you should," she says smirking, holding her foot out to me.

"No," I say harshly.

"Aw come on, I got a boo-boo" she taunts in a baby voice.

Yikes.

"Fine." I breathe out, preparing myself.

I lower myself to her foot and just as I'm about to kiss her clothed foot, she pulls away and gives me a look of disgust.

"Gross. I wasn't serious, you're so whipped it's honestly sad"

"I'm not whipped" I defend myself once again from her harsh remark.

"Right"

I pick her up and throw her onto the couch as she screams helplessly. A smile worked its way across her face and into her eyes.

There's something about her smile that drives me crazy. Ali just smiling could solve all of the world's problems in a matter of seconds. Even if the whole world was ending I'd still light up if I saw that smile, even during the last moments.

❤❤❤❤Authors Note

Shorter chapter but like anyways this chapter is very cute. Zaliyia 4ever!!!!! Not much to say but I'm impatient but I want this to kinda be a slow burn so let's hope I'm patient enough to make them kiss further in the book

17 | Volleyball Game

Aliyia

It's the last week of school before winter break and I am beyond excited. I'm not sure what my family has planned but we always do things for the Christmas holidays.

I am very nervous about tonight because we have our first volleyball game of the year and I'm just scared. It's not that I haven't done games before it's just that I always have a nervous breakdown the day, hour, and minute before.

Zayden can't make it though cause he has hockey practice and his coach is strict on missing practice unless you're dead.

Tate will obviously be there considering she's on the team with me so at least I'll have some support. And of course, my parents will come, hopefully. Aurora will be there I know for sure, she has never missed any of my volleyball games all my life.

Aurora is the best sister I could ever ask for. Although we have fits quite a lot, I love her unconditionally.

My palms have been sweaty all day just thinking about the game. Tate has reassured me multiple times telling me it's okay and we are going against one of the bad schools.

That doesn't stop my nervousness though, I can't help getting nervous sometimes even after being reassured multiple times.

Lunch swings by and I'm sitting in the cafeteria with Tate. Lukas and Zayden come out of nowhere and sit across from us.

Tate puts a fry in her mouth and shoots her boyfriend a glare.

"What?" Lukas asks confused about why his girlfriend is glaring at her.

"You ignored my text last night" Tate huffs.

"Oh, I was sleeping sorry love," Lukas says, trying to take one of her fries but she slaps his hand away.

"You read the message." She shoots back.

"Guys not this again, please go have your couples fight somewhere else" I groan. This is the second time this has happened this week.

I love them but I think they need couples counseling.

"Okay I'm sorry, I was playing games" Lukas admits.

Tate pauses for a moment then a smile crawls up her face and she speaks. "It's okay baby" and just like that, they kiss and make up.

"Ali, how are you holding up? I know you're freaked out about the game" Zayden asks me, taking one of my fries.

"Very nervous, and my palms have been sweating all morning," I tell him, rubbing my hands across my pants to dry them off.

"I know you'll do amazing, I believe in you," Zayden says, placing his hand on top of mine in a reassuring way.

I pull my hand away from his, not wanting him to feel the sweatiness of my palms. "Thanks" I reply dryly.

Zayden's expression turns dull after that. I feel bad but I can't stand it when people touch me while I'm sweating. It makes me feel gross and I don't want others getting grossed out by it.

Time went by faster than I wanted it to. The game was in less than thirty minutes and my palms are even more sweaty. My heartbeat is increasing by the minute, as my palms become the Pacific Ocean.

Volleyball has always been my passion. Before I decided I wanted to be a musician, I aimed for a professional volleyball player. Honestly, I'll make that my second resort if being a musician doesn't work out well.

"Allie" I hear a voice call out my nickname. It's Aurora.

'Allie' has always been a family nickname. My parents wanted to name me that but decided to name me something they could use Allie as a nickname for.

"Hey, Aurora" I greet, wiping my hands on my shorts once more.

"Don't be so nervous okay? Just remember the time ten-year-old you beat a fifteen-year-old volleyball player, that should keep you strong" Aurora says, rubbing my shoulder reassuringly.

The memory floods through my mind and I laugh at it. The look on everyone's faces when I did a 1v1 with that fifteen-year-old and won. She had a big ego tho, and she sucked.

"You'll do great" she reassures me once more before leaving the change room.

Ten minutes left. I'm going to kill myself right now just to skip this.

And there goes that increasing heartbeat feeling again. I should be happy about this but I don't understand why I'm more nervous and quiet than usual.

I was never scared of games when I was seven. I think my nervousness was triggered when I was thirteen and got smacked in the face with a ball at the start of the game. My nose broke due to pressure put on my face and I was bullied at school.

I was known as the "girl who can't bump" or "girl who can't set" to save her nose. Ever since I've been extremely nervous about games and have a fear that I will be smacked in the face with the ball and break my nose again.

"Aliyia, let's go it's time" one of my teammates calls out.

I slowly make my way out of the change room and hear the crowd cheering.

Fuck. Fuck. Fuck. Fuck. Fuck.

My breathing increased and I was about to have a panic attack until I felt a pair of hands wrap around me.

Zayden.

18 | Tickets

Aliya

Zayden is hugging me. I don't understand why he has hockey practice. He should be at practice not hugging me.

I think I'm imagining this. I blink once, then twice, until I'm repeatedly blinking. He doesn't let go. Zayden just stands there, lowering himself to my height and hugging me.

"What are you doing here?" I ask him, pulling away from him.

"I'm here for you" he responds, a smile crawling up his face.

"Why?" I question. "Don't you have hockey practice? And isn't your coach strict about missing practice without a good reason?"

"Yes but I had to see your first game, I couldn't miss it"

"But can't your coach bench you or something?"

"Technically yes, but he probably won't because I'm one of his best players. And I'm the captain too."

"Still-" I try to talk but get interrupted.

"That doesn't matter right now," he says bluntly. "What matters is that you get in there, and have fun. If you don't win it's not the end of the world, what matters is you have fun doing something you love."

"And don't worry about messing up, it's a part of life. Everyone messes up but they will always find their way back, trust me you will do amazing. I know you will beat those girls."

That was very motivational.

"Thank you, Zayden" I thank him, pulling him into a tight hug. I am very grateful to have him.

"Now get out there and kick their asses," Zayden says in between laughs.

Zayden's laugh causes my laugh to trigger and I laugh with him before heading to the game.

I have to serve first and I'm very scared I'll mess up but I remember what Zayden said. As I toss the ball up with my left hand and spike it with my right, it immediately flys above the net to the other side.

The girls on the other team didn't react fast enough because the volleyball reached the ground before they could dive for it.

Sudden cheers and applause from the crowd flooded through the room. It was mainly from Zayden, Lukas, Aurora, and my parents.

My biggest supporters.

My teammates hyped me up before getting into a new position.

Both teams are currently tied. It all comes down to this last round. The other team is starting with the ball.

As the player serves it, it comes in my direction causing me to immediately bump it up. I almost missed it.

The ball goes up in the air after a teammate sets it and I run up to spike it. When I spike it, it immediately travels to the other side and hits the ground.

We won. Half the crowd goes wild while the other half looks disappointed. Lukas, Zayden, Aurora, and my parents all stand up to cheer for me. A little embarrassing but it's fine, at least I have them supporting me.

My team surrounds me and cheers. The other team comes from the other side to congratulate us. One of the girls on the team gives me a disgusted look and returns to her friends who shoot me dirty looks.

All I did was smile at them.

Zayden and Lukas walk off the bleachers and head toward me and Tate who are talking.

"Good game ladies," Lukas says, bowing.

"Thank you, Lukas," I say, letting him go to his girlfriend to kiss her.

"You know that could be us," Zayden says, pointing at Lukas and Tate who are passionately kissing.

"Gross," I responded bluntly.

"Ouch" Zayden teases, putting a hand over his heart. "You did amazing"

"Thanks to you"

"Obviously thanks to me, I'm your favorite" he shoots me a wide grin.

"Mm I'm not so sure about that," I say laughing. He's not wrong, he quite literally is my favorite.

Maybe tied with Tate of course.

Bros before hoes.

"I have a surprise for you" Zayden blurts.

"What is it?" I ask, intrigued.

"Get changed first, I'll tell you after."

Uh okay.

I nod and head to change room, linking arms with Tate.

"What was that about?" She asks.

"I'm not sure"

After changing I exit the change room and search for Zayden. I find him sitting on the bleachers on his phone.

I secretly approach him from behind, wanting to scare him. "Boo!" I speak in his ear, in a loud voice.

His reaction was priceless. He jumped so hard, that he fell off the seat and landed on his ass.

I started laughing hysterically. That's the best reaction I've ever seen out in my sixteen years of living. Actually, that's a lie. I did it to my dad once while he was drinking milk and the milk started pouring out of his nose.

Disgusting.

"Fuck, you scared me," Zayden says, standing up.

"Oh shit really?" I taunt, it was quite obvious he was scared. "Are you going to tell me now? I have to go out with my family for a dinner."

"Yes, so basically" he pauses trying to find the right words. "I got the group tickets."

"You what?!" I spoke in excitement. "For where? When, how, why, what, who, AND WHAT."

"Chill. Hawaii, the day after Christmas break starts, the money I saved and my parents chipped in, because it's Christmas break and I love you guys, I got nothing for what it's just a vacation I guess, and for who, You, Lukas, Tate, and Me of course"

He said all that in one breath wow.

Excitement rose from the dead and I unwillingly jump up and down then jump on Zayden. Luckily he catches me and holds me close, being very careful about dropping me.

"Woah Woah Woah, calm down cheetah" Zayden laughs, setting me down gently.

"I just can't believe it, that's so soon. I need to pack, I need new clothes too" I speak all in one breath.

"Relax, we're all going to go shopping together this weekend," Zayden told me.

"Allie, let's go!" I hear my dad shout from across the court.

"I gotta go, I'll text you. But thank you!" I say once more before pulling him into a hug and departing from him.

"Oh how cute, are you guys dating?" Aurora smirks.

"No" I reply bluntly. I don't get why people keep thinking that.

"Yet," Aurora says in a teasing tone.

Aurora and her "yet" is honestly getting to my head. I swear she finds every little convenience between Zayden and I to haul us with questions on if we are dating or not.

"Congrats sweetie" My mom spoke, joy written all over her tone and expression.

"Thank you, mom"

"You did amazing, kiddo," My dad says with a smile before kissing my forehead.

It feels nice to have supportive family and friends, but it also feels great to win. Winning is my goal in life, I'm sure that's everyones.

You can always count on you're friends and family to support you. Or you can just get yourself a guy named Zayden Gryant.

❤❤❤❤Authors Note

EXCITING CHAPTERS COMING UP! And Aliyia is going to find out about the notes soon and the ACTUAL plot of the story begins. Don't expect a kiss till like chapter 29. But tbh I doubt I'd be able to hold myself back from that.

Quick hint, I'm thinking about making them get together at about 30 chapters in☐ not anytime soon depending on how many times a day I publish.

19 | Packing

Zayden

For whatever reason, I can't stop looking at the notes I found a few weeks ago. Aliyia still isn't aware I'm someone from her past.

I've been thinking of throwing hints to her so she can realize but that could also backfire. I know she has notes too, we promised to keep them with each other forever.

It's probably hidden away somewhere because I know she wouldn't break her promise that easily. Especially with someone who cherishes her so dearly.

Once I get her to figure it out, I wonder what she'll do. What if she gets angry at me for not telling her, she's always been the type of person to get mad for that. Only time will tell.

"Zayden snap out of it, we're at the mall now" Ali waves in my face. Guess I zoned out.

"I still can't believe you bought us tickets to fucking Hawaii!" Tate exclaims, exiting the car.

"Right, we can tan so much!" Ali exclaims as well.

Ali and Tate start rushing into the mall and heading to their favorite stores, leaving me and Lukas trailing behind them.

At this point, they are just dragging us around because we've been here for an hour and only the girls have bought items.

Mainly bathing suits, tees, shorts, and jewelry. They are also making us carry around their shopping bags as they continue shopping. For whatever reason, they keep on calling us whipped for this. I don't what it is with Ali and calling me whipped.

That's not true, I'm whipped for nobody but myself. Does that even make sense?

"Ladies, can we go shop for ourselves too?" Lukas groans, running his fingers through his hair.

"No," Tate says bluntly, not even glancing back at her boyfriend and focusing on the clothes in front of her on the rack.

"Can't you guys carry your stuff? We came here for us too" I say back furrowing my eyebrows in frustration.

Ali glances at me before speaking. "Fine, let us go to a few more stores then we'll let you guys shop"

A few more stores? They've been to practically all of them already. Lukas groans and sits on the couch beneath us.

The ladies finally let us hit up a couple of stores before we're all heading back to the car. "Whose house are we packing at?" I ask, getting into the passenger seat beside Lukas.

"Mine" Lukas replies, starting up his car.

"What about our suitcases?" Ali questions, scrolling through her phone. Her voice is soft and much less energetic than before.

"I have lots of them at my house, you can pack the rest of your stuff at home"

Ali nods and goes back to her phone. We did more shopping than we should've today, the trunk of the car can barely fit all the bags.

I'm the first one to exit the car as we pull up to Lukas's driveway. Lukas opens the trunk and everyone takes a portion of the bags before entering his house.

I'm pretty sure Ali has never been to his house before because once we enter she starts looking around like crazy.

Barking can be heard from the distance as it becomes louder.

Presh, Lukas's dachshund dog comes running straight to us and goes straight to Ali. Presh starts smelling Ali like crazy and starts licking her leg. Ali sets the bags down and bends down to pet Presh. She starts laughing a little when Presh licks her hand.

Her laugh, I wish I could listen to it forever. I always have to cherish and absorb her laugh because as quickly as it comes, it leaves just like that and she goes mute.

Ali isn't much of a talker around other people but around us, she shows so much of her true herself. I wish she could express her true herself around others.

Presh leaves us alone and lets us go up to Lukas's room.

Lukas gives each of us an extra suitcase to pack with. It's a smaller one since the trip isn't that long and we have other ones at home to use. This one is just for the clothing we bought today.

"Play some music," Tate tells her boyfriend who's folding a pair of shorts.

Lukas sets up his speakers and then blasts a Bruno Mars playlist. The guy has taste.

The girls start screaming the lyrics to "that's what I like" causing a chain reaction from me and Lukas as we both start screaming it with the girls.

We must've been way too distracted with singing because we did five percent packing and ninety-nine percent singing.

Ali suddenly stops singing and calms herself down before clearing her throat. "Guys we should finish packing first, I have to get home soon"

Everyone agrees and continues packing while singing softly.

Our flight is in two days and I've never been happier. I'm spending my Christmas break with the people I love most.

Second to my family of course.

❤❤❤❤Authors Note

This chapter is actually so boring I'm sorry LMAO anyways I've been gaining a lot more reads and I just wanna say I'm very grateful that this book is growing so quickly. I really hope I can fulfill your love story needs ▢

20 | Flight

Aliyia

It's flight day. I am going to fucking Hawaii today. I've always fantasized about living a dream life there after high school. I'm basically living that dream except for a shorter amount of time.

Zayden truly drives me wild the way he's always showing off. For whatever reason, I always end up enjoying it.

Since I wanted to be comfy on the flight I wore plain grey sweatpants and a blackish blue sweatshirt. I'm not a people pleaser but I still wanted to wear quite a bit of jewelry.

Not even to please people, I just can't go anywhere without wearing some sort of jewelry. Whether It's a necklace, a bracelet, or earrings.

Zayden's mom is picking us up and dropping us all off at the airport. I recently found out that Zayden's parents paid for all our parents and siblings to come to Hawaii a few days before Christmas so we aren't all on our own for Christmas.

I suddenly get a text from Zayden saying that everyone is outside in his mom's car and to come outside.

I quickly gather all my stuff and go to my sister's room to hug her then head downstairs. I put on my white converse and rush out the door with two suitcases.

I made sure to double-check last night, this morning, an hour ago, and five minutes ago that I had everything.

Zayden gets out of the car and helps me put my suitcases in the trunk of the van. It was jam-packed with suitcases but that didn't even surprise me. Zayden's family packed some things and told us to bring it with us.

Oh yeah, and Zayden's family owns a beach house in Hawaii. That's where we are staying for the break. Zayden showed us some pictures of it and the view is what I'm most excited about.

He said that sometimes he would go to the beach and watch the sunset. "A beautiful view to die for" is what he said.

Let's hope that it looks better in person.

The ride to the airport was silent. Not an awkward silence but just silent. We ended up talking in our group chat instead of in person even though we were all arms-length together.

We finally reach the airport and I am beyond excited. In just a couple of hours, I'm going to be in Hawaii. Fucking Hawaii.

Lukas messages the group chat saying "what if Zayden drowns at the beach" causing everyone to laugh except for Zayden.

"What's so funny?" Zaydens mom asks, pulling into an empty parking spot. "Yeah what's so funny?" Zayden shoots back with an annoyed tone.

"Nothing" Lukas, Tate, and I say in unison, holding back our laugh.

As we exit the car, we take our luggage and head straight for the airport. We check in, hand them our bags, and go through airport security before we are in the waiting area.

Two girls are sitting in front of us. One with blonde hair and one with black hair. They have been gawking their eyes at Zayden and Lukas ever since we sat down.

I whispered to Tate about it and when she looked up at them she saw the blonde winking at Lukas. Lukas saw it too because he looked at the blonde with a disgusted face and looked at his girlfriend.

Lukas pulled a smooth move because his arms swiftly wrapped themselves around Tate causing the blonde to scoff and turn in Zayden's direction. The other girl with black hair has had her attention on Zayden the entire time.

Her eyes never drifted from him. Zayden shifted uncomfortably and looked at me, his eyes saying do something.

It did annoy me how the blonde and the girl with black hair have been staring at Zayden like they'd like to have a passionate makeout session with him. Not that I'm jealous or anything.

I shift in my seat and purposely lean on Zayden's shoulder. He wraps his arms around me before leaning his head on mine.

Both the girls scoff loud enough for everyone around us to hear. Random strangers give those girls awkward, displeasing looks. Honestly, I understand why, they are one of the most annoying chicks I've seen in an airport and believe me I've seen way worse.

Two chicken wraps and soda later it's finally time for our flight.

"Flight to Hawaii is now available for boarding" Some lady on a speaker announces.

The chicks that were sitting in front of us stand up and collect their carry-ons. I think they're on our flight.

Of course, they have to be going to Hawaii, why else would they be sitting there. I just hope we never come across them ever again.

The group collects our carry-ons and goes straight to boarding. The seats on this plan were two per person in first class.

Tate sat with Lukas and Zayden sat with me directly behind me. And of course, the universe wants us to be tortured because those two girls from before sit directly behind Zayden and I.

As the ride begins, one of the girls starts kicking my seat. Straight out of a Disney movie. I try and ignore it but she keeps on doing it repeatedly like she wants me to lose my temper.

Just as I'm about to turn around and tell her off, Zayden covers my hand with his and shakes his head. "Don't, she's just looking for you're attention and a reason to make you mad"

Well, she's got that part right. She has my attention and she has certainly made me mad. I keep my cool and stay seated, ignoring the annoying kicking from behind me.

Eventually, she stops kicking when she realizes she's not getting a negative response anytime soon. I have people like that. Attention seekers like her can disappear from this world.

Only a few more hours left on this flight.

Authors Note

Hmm, should there be more appearances of those annoying girls? To create drama y'know anyways here is aliyias airport fit !

21 | Hawaii

Zayden

Hawaii. It's like my second home. Maybe third.

Only two hours of the flight to go. Not surprised that the airplane food is shit. It always is.

Ali is passed out asleep beside me. She's so adorable even when she sleeps. Bits of drool slowly become visible but randomly disappear.

I look away and stare at the beautiful cloudy sky before I hear a familiar voice speak. "Stop staring at me while I sleep, freak"

"Well good morning to you to sunshine"

"Fuck off"

A small laugh escapes from my lips as I turn my attention back to the cloudy sky. I receive a tap on the shoulder from someone who is not Ali.

I receive another tap and realize it's coming from behind. Not again. It's the blonde-haired girl. "Can I help you?"

"Yeah umm," she starts. "Are you dating that ugly chick beside you"

Before I can answer her Ali rises from her "slumber" and speaks for me. "Who the fuck are you calling ugly you gremlin,"

The blonde scoffs and snaps back. "Who else? You bitch."

Anger is written all over Ali's face as if she's been holding it in forever. "Are you trying to fight on a fucking airplane bitch because I seriously have no problem with doing that"

"Ali," I say trying to calm her down but she has a mind of her own and looks like she would take any type of reassuring at the moment.

"You don't know how long I've been waiting for this moment. It feels so fucking good to put a bitch in her place for once because she cannot keep her damn mouth shut. You have no right to go for another girl's man when it's been clear that they are in a relationship. So if I were you'd I'd back the fuck up before shit gets messy"

Damn.

That shut the blonde up because she looks out her window not saying a word. Wait did she say we were in a relationship.

"In a relationship huh" I glance at her scowling face.

"Shut up, I said what I had to"

It suddenly hits me. Jealousy? "Are you jealous or something?"

"What the fuck, no way. She was bothering both you and me so what I did was reasonable,"

"Could be jealousy though"

"It wasn't jealousy, she's just annoying"

"I can hear you, y'know," the blonde says from behind me.

"Good!" Ali shoots back. "Great, now I can't sleep anymore,"

I can't stop thinking about the possibility of Ali being jealous of that blonde. Not to be that guy but in my eyes, Ali is the most beautiful blonde I've ever seen. No other girl can compare.

Not even the most beautiful blonde, the most beautiful girl I've ever seen in my seventeen years of living. My eyes are always on her and never want to drift away. The day Ali realizes I'm her childhood friend is one of the days I'm scared for.

She could hate me, be annoyed with me, or end up falling in love with me. Though I'm sure she's starting that stage because I certainly am.

Lukas has already suspected it multiple times during practice and the number of times he catches me staring at her whenever the group hangs out.

Everything about her is so fascinating. Her eyes were captivating, by far the most attractive feature of her lit-up face. Her smile will always come first though. Some guys prefer the private parts of a female but those are the guys who never take the time to truly look at all the genuine features of a girl.

Time goes by quickly because the captain announces on the speaker that we will be landing soon.

As soon as the plane lands, old people start clapping. And only old people. The whole plant is silenced as about four people clap. A little awkward but they're just happy to be here.

"We're in Hawaii!" Ali exclaims loud enough for me to hear. She's pushing me out of the way to get a look out the window. Her hand is placed just above my belly button, pinning me to the chair.

She takes out her phone to snap a few pictures before returning to sitting as a normal person would sit.

People start getting up so that's exactly what Ali does. She moves and makes room for me to get out of my seat. I hand her carry-on to her and pick up mine. We follow Lukas and Tate out of the plane and thank the flight attendants.

"We're here!" Tate says jumping up and down in excitement.

"I know right, this is so exciting" Ali speaks, returning the same energy as Tate.

The air smells the same as I remember. Is that weird? A little.

After collecting our luggage, we grab a bite from the subway in the airport while waiting for our taxi driver. We had to request one with a van considering the load of luggage.

It was only a half-month trip yet we overpacked. You can never pack too much, who knows it might just come in handy.

Our taxi driver arrives and helps put all our luggage in the trunk. We have a car but it's at the beach house, we only ever use it every time we are in Hawaii. My family comes to Hawaii once or twice a year.

Like I said, my second or third home. I'll never forget Oregon though, that's my first home forever. I wish I could go back there and relive my childhood. It's sad to know that there's no to ever do that.

Did I mention my beach house was big? There are enough rooms to fit everyone that's coming and it has five bathrooms.

Rich family stuff.

I'm not surprised when I see the group's shocked faces as we pull up to my beach house. "What the fuck man, who know you were this rich" Lukas says, slapping my back.

I pay the taxi driver after we get all our stuff. I toss the house keys up in the air and smirk. "Are you guys ready for the best house tour of your life?" Their faces switch up and all three of them give me a disinterested look. Tate rolls her eyes and sighs. "Just open the door."

"Ok." I immediately respond by putting the key in the keyhole and unlocking the door. I'm the first to enter the house and it's just as clean as we left it this summer.

"Holy fuck" Lukas lets out as he enters the house, making space for Ali and Tate to enter. "You stay here like every break? Can your family adopt me, man?"

"No can do I can't deal with you and my little sister bro,"

Tate and Ali immediately drop their luggage from their hands and run straight to the kitchen island. Their eyes roam around the main floor of the house with sparkling eyes. Almost as if they've never seen or been to a beach house this big.

"Guys calm down, it's not that fascinating" I sigh as they make their way upstairs. Tate opens one of the guest bedrooms and her eyes sparkle brighter than ever. "I want this one!"

Ali groans immediately after Tate claimed the room "Fuck, I wanted this one.." Tate crashes on the bed and spreads herself in a starfish position. "Too late Aliyia, this baby is all mine"

Ali flips her off and goes to search for another room with me following alongside her. Lukas doesn't dare to follow us considering he's going to share with his girlfriend. "Don't worry, we have a better bedroom than that one" I whisper to Ali, watching her face light up with gleam.

"Show me"

I nod and lead her down the hall to the bedroom across from mine. "Just to let you know, this is my room so we'll be close to each other" I point to the bedroom across.

"Oh, great," She says sarcastically, rolling her eyes and putting her hand on the doorknob to open the room.

Her dull eyes quickly changed into a dazzled expression. The room was way bigger than the one Tate chose, with a lot more room space, a large bed, a big closet, and a mini-fridge.

The only reason these special things are in here is that our family likes to spoil any guest that comes here. And I may or may not have requested one of the people who watch this house while we're gone to put a mini-fridge in this room.

I was hoping the entire time Tate would pick the room she chose. This might be my excuse to get closer to Ali, what can I say. If you were in my position with the most beautiful girl, wouldn't you do the same?

She walks up to the bed and feels it up a little before opening the closet and mini-fridge. The look on her face brought a smile to my mouth. "I love it!" She yells maybe a little too loud.

"I'm glad you do, Ali. Anyways we should get the other and check out the beach" She nods and follows me out of the room, and down the hall.

I knock on Tate's door and get no response. I knock again and still get no response. Did they fall asleep already? "Guys we're coming in" I shout and knock once more with no answer.

Sighing to myself, I slowly turn the doorknob and open the door. My eyes have been corrupted.

I walk in to see Lukas and Tate engaged in a heavy make-out session. Lukas has his shirt off and has his hand lightly pressing on Tate's neck.

No words were able to escape my lips at the moment other than "okay then" as I quickly close the door. Ali is already bursting out laughing hysterically causing my laughter to arise. This happens every time she laughs, my body just feels the need to laugh with her.

Chain reaction type of shit.

"We haven't even been here for ten minutes and they're already getting freaky," Ali says in between laughs. They are little horn freaks, I've seen them make out before but I never wanted to experience walking in on them half-naked.

I loosen up and scratch my head. "I guess it's just you and me" She groans and clears her throat. "No shit, it'd be very disrespectful to their horn time if we made them come out with us"

Jeez, alright.

Sighing to myself once more before following behind her down the stairs. She slips on her white converse and ties up the laces as I do the same.

I open the door and move to the side waiting for her to step out. "Ladies first," Ali completely ignores my gentleman act and asks a question. "Are we walking or driving?"

Not that I would say this out loud to her but it's a beach house for a reason. "Walking, it's a beach house the beach is just down there"

Ali has a habit of rolling her eyes because every time I say a sentence she still finds the opportunity to roll her eyes. After rolling her eyes for the fifteenth in the fifteen minutes we've been here, she follows the direction I pointed to.

I honestly am just excited as them to be here.

Tate and Lukas are probably having the most fun at the moment.

I am still horrified by the sight. I don't think I'll ever recover.

❤❤❤❤Authors Note

I am going to give u a little spoiler for one of the upcoming chapters □

Ali finds out !!

LMAO THATS ALL U GET but yes Ali finds out □ lmk some of ur predictions on how she finds out, I want to see who get close

22 | Under The Sun

Aliyia

For the two hours I've been in Hawaii, I'm already in love with it. It's just as I always imagined it. Well, considering we are on the "rich" side of Hawaii. I'm very aware that there is a good and bad side to each country.

I wish I changed into my sandals before coming to the beach so I could feel the sand on my feet without the struggle of taking off my converse. Taking off converse is the worst thing ever. They just never want to come off.

The beach is not as crowded as I thought it would be. Only two or three families, old people, and I think one couple.

I can't get enough of the view. With my incredible senses, I can feel a pair of eyes going through the back of my head. I turn to Zayden and smile a little. "The view is beautiful"

"It really is," He said, staring directly into my eyes. Swimming sounds good right now, but I don't have my bathing suit on me and I don't want to get my clothes wet. And either way, it would be best to go swimming with the group. But Lukas and Tate are too busy getting freaky.

Like some romance movie or book, Zayden asks a question only the main love interest would ask. "Shall we take a stroll through the beach?" Of course, I cannot say no to that. I want to see more of this place anyways. "We shall."

Zayden leads the way, taking us to the right side of the beach. We pass by a few of the old people and shoot each of them small smiles.

"You're so lucky you get to come here for vacations and stuff," I said, looking at the waves before turning to look at him but he was already staring at me. "Well, I used to live somewhere else and I miss it there. Honestly, I wish we could go there for vacation instead."

He told me he used to live somewhere else but never told me where. "Oh, Where did you live before?" He looks up at the sky, then back at me, and prints a smile on his face. "Oregon"

No fucking way. My jaw drops to the floor and left walking beside this guy feeling speechless. How come he never told me this. And he knows I'm from there yet he never told me.

"Why didn't you tell me this before?" I ask, decreasing my walking speed. "Well, it just didn't cross my mind to tell you."

"But I told you I moved from Oregon, didn't that click any bells for you?"

Zayden sighs and shrugs. "I don't know Ali, it just didn't cross my mind okay?" He sounds frustrated now. Oops, I think I came off as harsh, but I mean it's not my fault is it? I wish he told me, who knows we could've been friends.

No, I doubt we were friends. I'm sure mine and his personalities would be different years ago. I think I'd hate a guy like him.

"Sorry" I mumble, taking one last glance at him before turning my attention back to the waves. Zayden doesn't speak for a while and we just walk along the beach in awkward silence.

Zayden breaks the awkward silence with a question that made my stomach rumble. "Do you want to grab a bite somewhere? I know a good place." Immediately yes.

My answer wasn't any less awkward than the silence before. "Uh, sure." That sounded quite rude. It just came out, I didn't mean it to sound rude or anything like that.

Okay, Zayden did not lie about this place being good. I just ordered one of their deluxe sandwiches and it's like heaven in my mouth. Whatever ingredients they used are just right. Enough seasoning, veggies, enough everything.

I have to stop myself from moaning at the delicious bite I just took. "This is fucking amazing," I say with a stuffed mouth.

Zayden furrows his eyes brows and looks at me weirdly. "Don't talk with your mouth stuffed, have manners." This bitch. I raise my hand and give him the middle finger, taking a sip of my Dr. Pepper drink.

Zayden leans back in his chair after taking a large sip of his sprite. "Should we get going soon? The sun is gonna set in a bit."

I nod in agreement and shoot him a fake half-smile. "Alright, give me a sec" I finish up the last piece of my heavenly sandwich, then chug the rest of my soda.

A beautiful waiter appears at our table and asks if we are ready for the check. She's way prettier than me, I can't even compete. She has beautiful long brown hair and blue eyes that compliment her perfectly.

She doesn't even pay any attention to me as she's at our table, she's looking at Zayden. Probably trying to seduce him with her beauty. But Zayden doesn't even give her a second look. He's looking at me with that perfect grin he always has painted on his face.

Before I can take out my card to pay, Zayden stops me and takes out his own. "My treat," he says, handing the card to the waiter at our table.

The waiter takes it gracefully and gives it back after a successful transaction. "So, can I have your number?" The waiter asks as she hands back his card.

Zayden doesn't even glance at her as he is still staring at me. "No," he answers so straightforwardly. Miss brunette scoffs and crosses her arms. "Why, do you have a girlfriend?"

"Doesn't matter if I do, I don't want you to have my number and that's that." He still isn't giving her another look and I'm pretty sure she noticed how he's staring at me because she scoffs and strolls away to another booth.

"Now that she's gone, shall we go?" He stands up from his seat and yawns slightly. His eyes never left mine that entire time. "Mhm," I mumble, getting up from my spot and following him out.

The sun has begun to set. And we're halfway back to the beach house before Zayden speaks up. "Hey, I'm sorry about before,"

I completely forgot everything that happened before so I'm confused. "What do you mean?" He sighs and looks away from me. "At the beach, I sounded irritated, I'm sorry.

The event reaches my mind and now that I think of it, it's not a big deal at all. It was just a tone, nothing serious. "Oh, that? That was nothing, it's fine."

"No, it's not just nothing. You looked upset and I felt so bad but I just couldn't find the right words to say anything about it, so I just stayed silent." He makes it sound as if he's guilty of something.

"Zayden it's fine. I promise you I don't care about that" I give him a reassuring smile as the sun sets lower. "But don't pay any attention to that, pay attention to this beautiful sun we're under"

He averts his attention from me and turns over to the sunset view. "This is the perfect view," he says, falling to the ground.

"Why'd you push me?" He asks, laughter being held back in his emotion. "Because I felt like it" I shoot back, sitting next to him.

"Let's just watch the sunset for a while, it's too beautiful to not watch," I say, getting in a comfortable position on the sand.

Zayden agrees and copies the position I'm in. Together we are under the sun, smiling, laughing, and talking. As if I would ever imagine this happening years ago. Little me would scream with joy right now.

Honestly, I've been holding back screaming with joy ever since the plane landed here. I would probably draw a lot of attention to myself by doing that either way.

I can't get enough of the sunset though. Probably the best sunset I've watched. "This sunset is really beautiful."

The next three words that came out of Zayden's mouth were completely unexpected. "You're more beautiful"

What. What. What. What. What. What. What.

How unexpected is that? He's never said that before. He's called me a "gremlin" or a "raccoon" but never "beautiful". Words can't even escape my mouth right now. I'm just left speechless. Although a genuine smile creeps its way onto my face unexpectedly. So many unexpected things have happened in the past couple of weeks.

"Oh" was all I was able to let out. I sound shitty for saying that but I seriously don't what to say. I've never been a responder, mainly a listener.

Zayden starts to laugh right after hearing my response."Wow, no thanks or anything"

"Fuck you, I don't what to say to that"

"A thanks would be great"

I sigh as I feel my body start to heat up. "Thanks."

"You're very much welcome," he said in an amused tone, he's always sounding amused it's not surprising.

I love this sunset. I love sunsets.

I love Hawaii.

❤❤❤❤Authors Note

Help I'm so sorry this chapter is so boring I had no ideas for this bro☐ anyways give me chapter ideas plz I have no ideas my chapters are getting boring srry bout that man.

Slow burn is killing the writer too guys

23 | Waves

Aliyia

I have the best idea ever. I make my way back to the living room with my friends after getting a glass of cold water. "Guys we should go surfing" I share. Zayden glares at me, his eyes saying "seriously?".

"Why are you looking at me like that, Zayden?" I question even though I know the reason. He can't swim. Swimming at a beach is worse than swimming in a pool. Because if you drown there's a possibility nobody will find your body and you will just float away for eternity.

Zayden rolls his eyes and leans back on the couch. "Because I can't swim, and you know that" Tate starts chuckling but covers her mouth before she goes ballistic.

"Alright, ill teach you how to swim" I added, sitting down next to him. "You're going to kill me," Zayden says, crossing his arms and scooting away from me. He's overreacting. Why would I try and kill my best friend? Well, there are reasons but I would never do it in a public area.

"I'm not going to kill you. Not in a public place at least" I joked. "But anyways since Zayden doesn't want to, we should all go" I added, chugging the water.

"Hey! I never said I didn't want to go, I just don't know how to swim." Zayden scoffed. Oops, my bad. But he didn't make that clear.

"Oh, my bad. But won't it be boring? You should just let me teach you how to swim please" I begged, interlocking my fingers with each other and displaying a begging face.

He looks as if he's considering it for a moment. A concerned expression was written all over his face. He's probably contemplating risking his life just to have fun or stay dry and safe without the possibility of death.

"Fine" he sputtered. I accidentally let out a yelp of excitement. "Yay, we should go now it's best at night" Zayden looks at me like I'm crazy after I said that. "Are you kidding me? Why night? What if I drown? Can we just go in the morning?"

It's better at night because there's nobody to bother you. Not like people will bother us but it's still enjoyable. I've always been a fan of night swims. "Because night swims are fun!" I exclaim.

"But" Zayden starts but gets cut off by Tate. "Dude if you don't want to then stay behind but I'm definitely in" Lukas agrees with his girlfriend and Zayden is left defenseless.

He groans and runs a hand through his hair before talking once more. "Fine, but if I die I will make sure all of you get sued and that's a promise"

"Yeah, Yeah, whatever let's go get our swimsuits now," I say, jumping off the couch and running to the stairs. Once in my new room, I make my way to my suitcase on the ground.

I haven't had time to unpack since I've been out and about pretty much all day. I look around the suitcase, messing it up a little as I look for a swimsuit. I find a bright pink plain bikini. This will do it. After I pick a pair of jean shorts to wear on top of the bottoms.

Perfect. I double-check myself in the mirror before turning off the lights and closing the room door. Coincidentally we all come out of our rooms at the same time. We are living in some movie I swear.

"It's beach time baby!" Lukas shouts, holding the waist of his girlfriend. I wish someone would hold my waist like that. Zayden moves closer to me and whispers something in my ear. "You know that could be us."

He's said this before, it's cheesy cute but kinda annoying. "Yeah, no." I bluntly say, walking away from him. Sure that must've been harsh but as much as I desperately want a lover, I'm still taking time for myself. "Ouch" I hear Zayden whisper from behind me.

❤❤❤❤Zayden

As we're walking to the beach, a lightbulb in my head turns brighter than ever. With this idea maybe I can get a few steps closer to making Ali realize who I am. "Ali" I call out to her, taking larger steps to reach her pace. "Yes?" I look at her, preparing my words.

"Have you ever had a childhood best friend in Oregon?" Of course, I know the answer to that but I want to hear it coming from her. She looks at me with a small smile plastered on her face. "Yeah, I did." She began.

"But he moved away when I was ten and I never saw him again. I feel so stupid for forgetting his name. I miss him and hope to see him one day. I hope he's doing good because I know when he left he had some type of family emergency. I never knew what it was though, I just hope he and his family are doing good."

She that all that in one breath I'm impressed. Everything but one thing she said was true. My family moved to New York because of some "family emergency". There was no family emergency other than my dad cheating on my mom with some nineteen-year-old.

My mother didn't want to stay in Oregon anymore because the thought of seeing him in public or making contact with him made her sick. She didn't want to tell anyone about it so she stated it was a family emergency.

We ended up staying with family in New York for a bit as they helped us settle down. My mom was able to find a good-paying job which led us to rent an apartment. Three years later my mom saved enough money to get us a good house. She found love again and was happier than ever.

That man is now my stepfather. I don't see him as much because he's always on business trips, but I know he's a good guy. He calls my mom twice a day while on a business trip to let her know everything he's done or going to do.

He's more of a father to me than my father ever was. And ever will be.

That's the true story.

"Did you have a childhood best friend in Oregon?" Ali asks, tucking both her hands in her back pocket. I want to say yes but the worst possible answer slips out of my mouth. "No, I didn't. I never really had friends back in Oregon."

"Then why'd you love it there so much?" She questions, pushing her hair behind her ear. The beach is like ten feet away from us but we're too engaged in our conversation to notice.

"Because even though I didn't have any friends, the memories I made there were amazing. And I was born there anyways" I lied a little. The only lie in that sentence was that I didn't have any friends. I had Ali. But I lied.

Why are the lies slipping out so easily? I hated the fact that I'm lying to her but it was too late to take it back now. She nods and her smile spreads when she feels the sand on her feet.

It's dark out and the beach is empty. Not surprisingly, it's almost 10:20 pm. "You're still teaching me how to swim right?" I ask, setting the large blanket I brought down on the ground. "Of course I am" she sets down her bag on the blanket and smiles.

Her smile is so addicting. The most beautiful smile I've ever seen.

After settling down a little, we all race to the water. Ali pushes me into the water and laughs evilly as she does so. I get up and pick her up only to throw her in. "We should have a chicken fight" Tate suggests, moving closer to her boyfriend.

"Alright me and Ali against you two," I say picking Ali up and throwing her over my shoulders. I'm trying to be careful so I don't drop her, my hands holding her thighs tightly but not in a way she'll feel any pain.

Lukas and Tate copy us and soon the girls are trying to push each other down. One thing I know about Ali is she won't back down. And of course, she didn't back down because we won. She used all her strength in one push and pushed Tate causing Lukas to stumble and fall into the water.

"Woo!" She exclaims, putting her hands up in the air. I let her down and give her a double high five. "We are so pro," I tell her, looking back at Lukas and Tate to see her scolding him about keeping his feet planted on the ground.

Mine and Ali's laughs echo through the beach as Tate and Lukas look back at us and begin laughing with us.

Ali looks at me and grabs my wrist pulling me deeper into the water. "Okay time to teach you how to swim" I'm a bit hesitant to do this but she's committed to teaching me so I won't fight back for now. "Just watch me"

She smiles at me before showing me her swimming moves. "It's honestly simple. just don't freak out and keep on moving your feet" She shows me once more before encouraging me to try. Fuck I'm gonna die from this.

I try and copy her movements but sink immediately after. She helps me up and I can see the held-back laughter in her expression. "That's okay, try again, and don't freak out. That's why you sunk" I listen to her words carefully and take a big breath before attempting again.

This time I lasted a little longer and I moved a couple of centimeters. When I reached the surface again Ali clapped her hands in approval. "Good job, you're improving."

We do this a couple more times until I'm capable of doing it without her help. I discreetly swim to a making out Tate and Lukas and grab Lukas by his leg, pulling him down.

Ali laughs at the sight causing Tate to run and push her down in the water. But Ali is smarter than that and drags Tate down with her. Most of our night is spent pushing each other down.

"Alright guys we're gonna head out now," Tate says and heads towards the shore, Ali following beside her.

"Just look at our girl's man" Lukas puts an arm around my shoulder and eyes his girlfriend down from the back. "You and Aliyia are dating right bro?" I wish I could say yes to that.

"Not yet."

❤❤❤❤Authors Note

A longer chapter I guess also no outfit inspo for u☐☐ just imagine a plain bikini and jean shorts on top guys she's gonna find out rlly soon☐

24 | Coke and Mentos

Aliyia

I'm the only friend who has amazing ideas because I just got another fun idea we could do. Although I should wait till everyone is awake. It's only 11:30 am but I'm pretty sure everyone is still passed out.

One lucky thing about my room is it has a balcony. I don't understand why Zayden saved me this room out of all the other ones. He honestly is the most whipped person I've ever met.

Getting up from my comfy bed, I slip on some slippers and head to the balcony. The fresh Hawaii air is everything. If I could live here every day for the rest of my life I would.

I hope I can live here with my significant other one day. Or maybe own a beach house like this with whoever I end up with.

My phone dings from the bedroom and I leave the balcony to go check who it's from. Zayden, why is he up? I thought he would be asleep right now.

zayden ☐

Z: are you up?

Me: yeah, why?

Z: can you come down?

Me: I could but why?

Z: please

Me: fine u gremlinread 11:34 am

Wow, the bitch really left me on read. Why is he calling me downstairs at 11 am? He makes it sound serious.

I open my door and notice Zayden's room door slightly open. I know I shouldn't but I peek through the gap and see a box on his bed.

Not that it's any of my business but I'm really curious. Maybe he ordered something off amazon. The door slightly creaks as I open it but not loud enough for someone downstairs to hear.

As I approach the bed I see a bunch of letters and little notes in one pile. Huh? How weird. Why does he have so many letters and notes?

Once again, curiosity flows through me and I have the urge to look at one of the letters. Just before I can pick one up, Zayden comes in the room. Shit.

"What are you doing?" He asks, coming closer to me. "Oh, I saw a box on your bed and was curious to see what it was." There's no point in lying since I was already caught.

"What are those?" I point to the piles of papers inside the box.

"Just old papers from my childhood, nothing important," he said, running a hand through his hair. I thought he would be mad at me for snooping around. "Aren't you mad at me for snooping?"

He looks at me a small grin appears on his face. "I could never be mad at you"

That's surprising. "Oh, well what did you want me to meet you downstairs for?"

"I was thinking we could have a movie marathon with the others when they wake up," he says, sitting on the edge of his bed.

No way the guy read my mind. That was originally the idea I had planned in my head.

But Couldn't he just wait till everyone was awake? "Why couldn't we do that when the others were awake?"

A sudden smirk shows up on his face. "Well I was thinking we could wake them up with a little.." he pauses. "Fun?"

Even though I don't know what his meaning of fun is, a smirk appears on my face and we're both looking at each other with evil grins.

"Shall we?" He says standing up and sticking his hand out for me to grab. "We shall," I grab his hand and follow him downstairs.

"What's the plan?" I ask, watching him fill up cups with water. He sets one of the cups down and grabs a coke bottle from the fridge. "Coke and Mentos thing, plus water just in case" He gets a package of mentos from the pantry and smiles.

I don't remember needing water for the coke and mentos thing but I guess I'll let it slide. It's weird though. He hands me the coke bottle and points to the stairs.

We both quietly make our way upstairs and stop at Tate's room door. Just before Zayden opens the door, he looks at me and smiles before shushing me up. I didn't even say anything but alright.

When he opens the door, we see a spooning Lukas and Tate. They're both sound asleep. From what I can see, they're both in deep sleep. Zayden goes to the other side of the bed and gestures for me to lean the bottle towards him.

In one swift movement, Zayden slips the mentos into the bottle and quickly shuts up with the cap. I shake it and point the bottle at them, backing away a little. Zayden holds the bottle and opens the cap, the liquid exploding onto Tate and Lukas.

As they're waking up, Zayden hands me two cups full of water and whispers for me to pour it on them. They both fully wake up from the water. "What the hell?" Tate yells shooting up from her laying position.

Zayden and I burst into uncontrollable laughter when we see the looks on their faces. Zayden falls to the ground and grabs my shirt to pull me down with him causing me to land on his chest.

"Fuck you guys, now we're sticky," Lukas said while trying to dry himself off with a towel. In sync, Zayden and I look at each other and our laughs return. "You should've seen the looks on your faces," I say out of breath.

Tate glares at me and runs a towel through her hair. "It's not funny." Oh but yes it is. But to be fair, it wasn't my idea.

And I guess it was a little uncalled for but they can't lie, it was funny. Maybe not the joke itself, but the look on their faces was priceless.

"Meet us downstairs when you're done cleaning the... stickiness off you," Zayden says before grabbing my wrist and pulling me out of the room while laughing.

"You're evil," I tell him, crashing onto the couch. Zayden sits beside me, still laughing uncontrollably. Weird to think about but his laugh is contagious. And adorable.

For the whole tough guy act at school, he laughs like a kid. It's cute.

I just realized I never took much notice of his eyes. Only when I first met him. The green and blue eyes of his shined brighter than a diamond. I never paid much attention to his eyes, that's why I forgot he has heterochromia.

I've only met one other person with heterochromia and that was at a grocery store when I was seven years old. But the woman was gorgeous, not only in her eyes. I won't lie, I was jealous of her eyes. I begged my mom to let me dye my eyes like that.

Yes, I thought you could change your eye color just like that. I thought you could dye them like you dye your hair. An idiotic thing to think but what can I say? I was seven.

"Take a picture, it lasts longer." Oh wow, what a cliche thing to say. But shit, he caught me staring. "What for?" I try acting clueless but it's pretty obvious I was staring.

Zayden scoots closer to me and didn't break eye contact. "You know what. You were staring" why does he have to say it like that. "No, I wasn't."

He tilts his head slightly and pokes his inner cheek with his tongue, holy shit. "No need to be shy Ali, I don't mind." Why does he have to sound so hot? Oh my lord.

"Whatever" I sigh and lean back on the chair.

❤❤❤❤Authors Note

This is one of the chapters I actually like but then again it's kinda weird. writing is so tiring.

movie marathon chapter next !! also, what r ur opinions on flirty zayden ;))

25 | Movie Marathon

Z ayden

Ali and I are talking about how great sushi is when Tate and Lukas come downstairs. They're both glaring at us like crazy as they come our way. "Hey guys," Ali said, smiling like a cute idiot. That fucking smile.

"Stop" Tate glares and sits down on her boyfriend's lap. Ali drops her jaw and shoots her hands up in defense. "What did I do?!"

Tate shifts around and pulls Ali by the ear towards her. "You know what you did." Ali throws her hands up in defense again and moves away from Tate, coming closer to me.

"Anyways" I start. "What movie should we watch? I'm thinking we should watch the Marvel movies in order."

"Yeah, we should" Ali immediately agrees, a smile reaching her face. For fucks sake why does her smile send chills up my body? Not the bad chills where you feel like someone is stalking you or bad vibes. The chills where you feel your body burst into a million pieces out of happiness.

Words can not explain how many good chills Ali gives me.

"Whatever" Tate said, tucking her head in Lukas's neck. Alright, then lovebirds.

Ali goes on her phone and by the looks of it, she's on an illegal website. Seconds later, a movie was projected onto the tv, the intro of a movie playing. She probably hooked it up from the website.

Ali stands up and brushes off invisible dust on her shorts. "I'm going to go get popcorn and get drinks, I've already watched this movie anyways."

After she disappeared into the kitchen, I stood up and followed her direction. I've seen the movie way too many times. Summer always makes me rewatch marvel movies with her. I almost know some of the script by heart.

As I enter the kitchen I see Ali leaning on the counter beside the microwave. The popcorn is popping in the microwave loudly.

I must've stared for too long because she turned around and met my gaze. "What are you doing?" She asked, looking at him with a soft face. There's no point in lying, especially when I want her to realize that I am her childhood best friend.

"Watching you."

Her cheeks tinted red as she drifted from my gaze, finding a spot on the floor to look at. "That's weird," she tells me, averting her attention from the floor back to my eyes.

I can't stop looking at her. It's like every time I look at her I get sucked in by her spell. Anytime I catch even a glance at her I feel like

I'm swimming through an emerald green pool of water, never finding a shore.

Ali walks up to me and punches my shoulder. "Stop staring at me, it's weird." The way she punched my shoulder was cute. The way I didn't feel anything from that punch was cute. "And if I don't stop staring? What'll happen?"

Her eyes keep looking from the floor to my eyes, back and forth. And even though we are only two inches apart, I feel as if I'm being drawn closer to her by the second. "Zayden." She whispered softly, moving closer to me, closing the space between us.

"Yeah?" I tilt my head slightly, staring at her emerald green eyes that stared back into mine. I swear I could see a small spark in her eyes before they were quickly washed away.

"The popcorn is ready, take it out." Just as she said that the microwave went off and started beeping repeatedly meaning the popcorn was ready. Did she have to tease me like that?

Ali backed away with a knowingly smirk on her face, as she turned and walked got the fridge. She knew what she was doing there, and whatever it was it worked.

I curse under my breath and go straight to the popcorn, doing exactly as she told me.

Ali was grabbing drinks from the fridge and a few cups. "Good to know that you're doing what I told you too, whipped boy." God, why does everyone think that I'm whipped? "For the last time, I'm not whipped, Ali."

She hummed and smiled to herself before walking back to the living room. "Yeah, whatever you say, Zay." Did she just call me Zay? I can feel my heart jump up and down in my body. My heart is spinning around with excitement, I think it might burst.

My head was somewhere else because as I was pouring the popcorn into a bowl, half a portion of it spilled on the floor. Shit.

I don't even have time to react fast enough because Ali comes back to the kitchen. And as she was opening her mouth to say something, she paused when she saw the mess on the floor. A laugh escaped from her lips as she desperately tried covering it up with her hands.

"Sorry to burst your bubble Zayden but there is a popcorn spill on aisle one." She joked. No matter how hard I tried, I couldn't stop myself from laughing at her jokes. Sometimes, they aren't even that funny. She just amuses me in every way possible that I let out a real laugh every time.

Fuck, what is she doing to me?

Multiple movies later, we are on Avengers Endgame and tears are falling out of both Tates and Ali's eyes. They're cuddled up close to each other, sobbing with their popcorn lying scattered on their shared blanket.

Lukas looks at me then at his girl then back at me. I scratch my head and shrug my shoulders, speaking to him without words.

As the end credits play, Ali and Tate are officially sobbing messes. If I was an award person, I would reward them for crying the most during the ending of an avengers movie.

Lukas copies my movements from early and scratches his head, looking at the sobbing girls.

"Ladies, it's okay" he tries putting a reassuring hand on Tate's back but she immediately pushes it away, cuddling up closer to Ali.

Lukas shoots me a "well I tried look" before standing up and grabbing all the bowls. I stand up with him and pick up the drinks and cups, following him to the kitchen.

Lukas places the bowls in the sink and leans on the counter afterward. "So, how's it going with you and Ali?" That's some strong language he's using there.

"Okay one thing, only I can call her that nickname," Lukas lets out a laugh and throws his hands up in defense. "My bad man, I meant Aliyia." Good. "Well, things are going too slow. I feel like I'm in some slow-burn teenage movie."

Lukas looks at me and sighs, a grin suddenly appearing on his face. "So, how the fuck do you comfort a girl crying over the ending of an avengers movie?"

One thing came to mind. My mom always used to do this when she was grieving over a tv character or literally anything.

"Ice cream."

❤❤❤❤Authors Note

Thoughts on this chapter? Always what do u think about Ali teasing him she doesn't know yet ofc but she just finds it funny to tease him. Also bear with me, I hate how slow this slow burn is too trust me. But I'm gonna cave in and make them kiss soon I promise

26 | Family

Zayden

Our families are coming today. I'm pretty sure they are on their last flight at the moment. They are most likely gonna arrive sometime at six pm so we decided to surprise them with dinner. Lukas is washing dishes, Tate and Ali are cooking the main course, and I'm in charge of the appetizers.

We went shopping a couple of hours before and got things we'd need for tonight and for some of our stay. I paid a good $236.67 for everything. Groceries do not come for cheap. But we did get a lot anyways.

"What's the main course, ladies?" Lukas asks, rinsing off one of the dishes.

The girls look at each other, a smile on both of their faces. "Well we were thinking pasta, it's a classic but you can never go wrong with it," Ali says, pushing Lukas to the side so she can put water in the pot.

Tate grabs a few boxes of pasta from the grocery bag and sets them on the counter. "What type of pasta did you guys get?" I ask.

Ali looks at me, her eyes dimmer than usual. "Rigatoni and Fettuc-cine, we're gonna serve both and they can eat whichever they want."

I hum and go through the bag to find ingredients for my mozzarella cheese. All I need is mozzarella cheese, eggs, and bread crumbs. That's how I usually make them anyways, it's quick and easy.

Ali approaches me and looks over my shoulder."Need help? I'm waiting for the water to boil anyways" I turn my head to look down at her and smile at her. "Sure, can you cut the mozzarella into little squares?"

She nods and grabs a knife from the knife rack. As she's cutting the cheese I'm preparing the eggs, putting a couple of eggs into one bowl and mixing it up well. After, I pour the bread crumbs into a bowl.

As I'm pouring the crumbs into a bowl, I hear a yelp come from beside me. I turn my head to look for the sound and see Ali sucking on her finger.

"What happened?" I question, my eyes trailing from her finger in her mouth to the blood on the knife. It's not like it was a heavy amount of blood but it was more than there should be for a knife cut.

"I cut my finger" Ali looks at me, removing her finger from her mouth but still seeing blood gush out. Luckily my mom has a safety kit thing around the house. One time Summer was being stupid and almost chopped off her entire finger. I wish I was joking.

I bend down to open the cabinet below me and pull out an emer-gency kit. Might be a little too extra for a knife cut, but my mom always says "never risk it". I always follow those words.

I clear the space on the counter and tap on it, trying to signal her to sit on top. She doesn't get what I'm saying so I pick her up by the waist and set her on the countertop. "Let me take care of you,"

Reaching for the bag, I unzip it and take out swabs and rubbing alcohol. I pour some of the rubbing alcohol on one of the swabs and gently place it on Ali's cut.

She winces in pain and I stop to look at her before continuing. I can hear her breathing increase by the second. Her body is almost pressed against mine, a few centimeters keeping us apart.

I make sure to scan her expression carefully while cleaning her cut. Her eyes stare into mine while mine stares into hers, neither of us daring to say a word.

Throwing the swab in the garbage, I grab a band-aid from the bag and softly put it on while still making eye contact with her.

"There you go" I back away to ease the tension between us. Ali jumps down from the counter and smiles. "thank you." I know she was flustered from that. The way she didn't say a word and the way I could hear her heavy breathing meant she was flustered. Or possibly nervous I guess.

"The waters ready" I point to the boiling water on the stove. I continue cutting the cheese while Ali puts the pasta in the water, and Tate and Lukas are doing God knows what.

"Tate and Lukas get your butts down here and be useful!" Ali yells. A couple of seconds later, Lukas and Tate both come running down the stairs with messy hair.

"Come on guys there are plenty of opportunities to do that and now is not one, we need to finish this before they get here," Ali said, rolling her eyes.

Dinner is ready and we're on our way to the airport. We only have one available seat meaning everyone else would have to take a cab. I'm thinking we should take my sister summer or Ali's sister Aurora. Most like Aurora because she fits more in our age group.

I pull up to an available parking slot and unbuckle my seat belt. "To our families, we go," I say, exiting the car. Ali stares at me weirdly and scrunches up her face. "That's so cringy."

Ignoring her harsh words, I third wheel behind Tate and Lukas who has his arm around her. Realizing they aren't going to acknowledge I'm there anytime soon, I awkwardly walk beside Ali. "Are you excited?" I ask her, entering the airport.

"Yeah, I am" her answer sounded dull. She looked drained and annoyed. Something is definitely bothering her. "Hey is everything okay?"

She looks at me weirdly, scrunching up her face again and shrugging. "Yeah everything's okay, why wouldn't it be?"

"Well, you just seem like there's a lack of interest in you, plus you look pissed off."

She sighs as we reach the waiting room. "Well, I found out the guy I like is dating one of those perfect cheerleaders."

My heart drops to the ground. Why didn't I know that she liked someone? Who does she even like? "Oh, who do you like?"

"Football captain, Karter Shoupe" I hold back a laugh. That boy is a certified player. He hooks up with anyone that breathes or every blonde. If you're lucky, maybe some brunettes. And rarely any red-heads.

"Why Karter?" I genuinely question. What does she see in him that's so special. I'm surprised she hasn't caught on to his whole player act.

Before she can answer someone shouts her name. "Aliyia!" It's her sister, Aurora. She's running up to her with open arms, leaving her luggage behind her. Ali gets up from her seat and runs to her sister to hug her.

"Hi, Rora. How have you been?" Ali says pulling away from the hug. Funny, I've never heard Ali call her sister that nickname.

Soon enough, Lukas's parents come down the escalator, then Tate's, then finally my mom and my stepdad. Summer included.

My mom runs up to me and throws her arms around me. "My sweet boy, how have you been?" I haven't always been fond of the nickname "sweet boy", especially in public. It's okay when she addresses me like that in private but in public it's quite embarrassing.

"I've been good mom, how about you?" I pull back and smile at my stepdad and sister behind her. "I've been good too, my dear." Her eyes averted from me to my friends who were greeting their parents.

Her eyes widened when she saw Ali's mom. "Lindsey?" Fuck, I kinda forgot to tell her about Ali's mom.

They know each other because they were best friends before we moved to New York. Lindsey, Ali's mom drifted from Ali and turned to look at my mom. Her eyes widened as well. "Amaya?"

Ali looked at me confused and I gave her a confused look as well. I knew exactly what was happening, best friend reunion after like six years, but I didn't show I knew. Ali walked up to them and gave them both a confused look. "How do you guys know each other?" She asked but was ignored.

"Oh it's so good to see you again Lindsey," my mom said, pulling Ali's mom into a tight hug. All eyes were on them and only three truly knew what was happening. Me, Summer, and my StepDad, Trae.

"It's a long story everyone, we can discuss it later but let's start going now," Lindsey announced, pulling away from my mom. Ali turns her body to face mine and crossed her arms. "Zayden, how come you never told me our moms knew each other?"

Because I was waiting for you to figure it out. "I didn't know they knew each other either" I lie. Lie after lie.

Her eyebrows shoot up as she searches my face. Let's just hope I don't look guilty right now. "Well, alright" she sighs and walks away.

Close one.

I doubt she'll find out anytime soon. And I would love to keep it that way, at least just for a little longer.

❤❤❤❤Authors Note

PREDICTIONS FOR THE NEXT CHAPTER ->>

Foreshadowing??? Maybeee. Hope u enjoyed this chapter, also I recommend a seatbelt for next chapter :)

27 | Confused

Aliyia

The fact that my mom and Zayden's mom know each other lingers in my mind. Zayden and I never introduced them to each other so how come they act as if they were best friends?

I'm seated in the passenger seat beside Zayden. Tate, Lukas, and Aurora were seated in the back. So far, Aurora has gotten along with us. Probably because she's closer in age to us.

Of course, I love Summer, but she's newly thirteen and the rest of us are turning seventeen and eighteen. That starts lingering in my mind too. Zayden's eighteenth birthday is in less than a month on January 15th.

Zayden pulls up in the driveway of the beach house. A couple of seconds later an Uber appears. Then a second one, then a third. Everyone is here.

The adults greet each other for what feels like hours and leave us kids to carry their stuff inside. Zayden sighs and wipes imaginary sweat off his forehead. "Can't believe they're chatting for so long that they make us carry their bags" fact.

The fact that Zayden's mom and my mom know each other won't leave my head. I also have a suspicion that Zayden is lying about knowing that they knew each other. But then again, why would he lie to me?

I don't think he's ever lied to me and I appreciate that. I love when he's honest.

"Yeah, man" Lukas agrees, plopping down on the couch. Soon after, the adults pile into the house, meeting us in the living room.

My mom immediately comes my way, her attention on Zayden. "Oh Zayden, you've grown so much these past years" what? What does she mean by that?

Zayden's face turned pale and his chest started moving faster. Why is he reacting like that? He doesn't look like he's gonna speak up anytime soon so I say something instead. "What do you mean, mom? How do you know him?"

My mom looks at me like I'm stupid and tilts her head. "Aliyia, dear, how do you not know? Zayden was-" she was cut off by Zayden before she could finish. "We have a surprise for you guys, we need everyone to get dressed in their fanciest outfits they brought."

His pale skin started to fade lightly. What is going on? My mom was completely lost in everything she was about to say because she ignored everything that was going on before. "Oh that's wonderful," she says, turning away to her bag.

What the actual fuck? So she just forgot about everything? She was about to tell me something about Zayden. What did she mean by he's grown up? This is all so confusing.

A thought lights up in my mind but immediately goes away. No way, that's impossible.

Is it?

An hour later I'm staring at myself in the mirror in my room. My outfit was just a brown long-sleeved dress that hugged my body perfectly.

I definitely didn't wear the fanciest outfit I had but half the time I was supposed to use to get ready was spent thinking about a million possibilities on how my mom is familiar with Zayden.

As I was applying my mascara there was a knock on my door. "Come in!" I shout, continuing to gently apply the mascara to my lashes. The door opens and I can see Zayden through my mirror reflection, standing in a black suit. "Hi," I say, looking away to finish my mascara.

"Hi," he says back, leaning against the doorway with his hands in his pockets. When I'm done with my mascara I set it back in the makeup bag and turn to look at Zayden who's still standing in the doorway with his hands in his pockets.

His eyes scan my frame, shimmering light in his eyes. "So? How do I look?" I ask, twirling around with a big smile plastered on my face.

Zayden's lips curl up into a smile and he looks me in his eyes. I don't know why he always looks in my eyes. And I don't know why I always like it when he looks at my eyes like that.

"You look beautiful, Ali" fuck, why does he have to say it like that? I turn my head around to avoid facing him with my picking-up heartbeat. I can hear him step closer to me until we are just a few inches away.

His eyes go from my eyes, to lips, and back to my eyes. I want to look away, but I can't. I just stare back at him, with glimmering eyes.

Luckily, he looks away first, a wide grin on his face and lit up cheeks. Was he flustered or something? "You have something on your face," he tells me, looking back at me but this time at my cheek then back to my eyes.

Zayden uses his thumb to wipe something off my cheek, never breaking eye contact with me. He rubs his fingers together in an attempt to get whatever was on my cheek off. "All good, are you ready?" He asks me.

I was too lost in his eyes to answer. "Ali?" He calls out to me, shifting slightly. That gets my attention. "Oh, yeah sorry." How embarrassing.

"Well then." He clears his throat and lifts his arms. "Shall we?" I look up at his arms that are just waiting for me to link with him. A smile crawls up on my face as I link with him.

"We shall."

❤❤❤❤Authors Note

I love them sm and they are my characters bro anyways prepare yourselves guys, the next few chapters are... well that's a spoiler so just read and see ;)

Here's Ali's dressss

28 | Truth

Aliyia

Zayden and I make our way downstairs, our arms linked. I guess we were the last ones because everyone was seated at the empty table. I unlink my arms with Zayden and sit beside Tate, Zayden sitting beside Lukas directly across from me.

My dad clears his throat before speaking. "So what's the surprise you kids have for us?" The four of us look at each other and smile before getting up to walk to the kitchen without saying a word.

It takes us about five minutes to make sure everything is heated up and warm before returning to the dining room. Zayden's mom's eyes widen and she covers her mouth with both of her hands. "Oh my God, you kids did this for us?"

Zayden grins and nods at her, setting down the rigatoni pasta while I set down the fettuccine pasta. Aurora doesn't seem impressed but I can see the little light in her eyes.

Lukas sets down the dishes and Tate sets down the appetizer. Lukas disappears for a moment and then returns with drinks. Champagne for the adults and soda for the rest of us.

"Oh wow, this is wonderful." My mom exclaims, clasping her hands together. I smile at her and then turn to look at Zayden who's already looking at me with his green and blue eyes. The most perfect eyes I've ever seen.

Zayden breaks eye contact first to look over at the adults who are pouring themselves a glass of champagne. "Feel free to dish as much as you want for yourself." He sounds so professional.

Summer immediately grabs a plate and starts dishing out the fettuccine pasta before placing two mozzarella sticks onto the plate as well.

A few minutes later, everyone has dished their food and is eating. "Wow, this is really good." Tate's mom tells us. Tate smiles at her and speaks. "Thanks, mom, I made that one." She points at the rigatoni pasta.

Something that hasn't popped up in my mind for a while finally does. Zayden and my mom. I think I should ask about it.

Should I?

I want to know. No, I need to know.

"Hey, mom" I pick at my food with my fork and look up at her. She answers with a "yes dear" before taking a bite from her pasta.

Here goes nothing. "Earlier you were going to tell me how you knew Zayden, could you tell me know?" I glance at Zayden to see him frozen in place.

"Oh, you don't know dear?" Zayden's mom looks at me with confusion written all over her face. Almost as if I'm stupid. "Know what?" I question, all eyes were on me now.

Except for Zayden who's intensely staring at his food.

My mom wipes her mouth with a napkin before looking at me. "Well I'm surprised you don't know but when you were little-" once again, she's cut off by Zayden.

"Do you really think we have to talk about this right now? How about we just enjoy this dinner instead." He sounds worried about something.

I look at him weirdly, he's hiding something. "Why do you keep interrupting her?" I refer to my mom, slightly raising my voice. He picks at his food before looking at me with dim eyes. "It's just that we don't need to talk about this right now."

All eyes are on both of us while we both stare at each other. "Are you hiding something from me Zayden?" My voice raises a little higher than I wanted it to. But I'm so frustrated right now, something is going on and I need to know.

"No it's just," he pauses, his eyes falling back to his pasta. He doesn't say anything. "It's just what, Zayden?" He sighs and his eyes meet mine. "Complicated" he finishes.

I scoff and turn back at my mom who's looking at both of us weird-ly. "Mom tell me, please" I need to know now, especially since he's hiding something from me. "No, please don't," Zayden says quietly.

Lukas and Tate are looking at us with confusion, Summer not so much. And Aurora is covering her mouth with her hand, trying to contain her laughter.

"Yes mom, tell me please!" I don't mean to raise my voice at my mom but it just slips out like that, I don't mean it. My mom looks at me offended, most likely because I just raised my voice at her.

Zayden tries to say something again but I interrupt him before he can let the word out. "Please," I need to know now and it's killing me.

I look at Zayden but this time with sincere eyes. "Zayden, why won't you tell me? What's so bad about it?" He returns the same sincere expression. "I don't want you to be mad"

Oh really? "If you don't want me to be mad then I suggest you let my mom tell me or you tell me instead." Zayden looks at my mom and then back at me. He sticks his finger out, indicating for me to wait before retreating upstairs.

A minute later he comes back, something stuffed in his hand. "What is that? I ask, my gaze on whatever's in his hand.

He sighs and hands it to me, looking away from me. I take it from his hand to see it's a small piece of paper that's folded, I unfold it and notice writing on it.

I slowly read it and boy am I shocked.

Karter is so mean to me. He keeps yelling at me for messing up :(I just want him to move schools. I cant stand him.. also I have a sandwhich for lunch and a juice box

-Liyia

How does he even have this? I wrote this when I was like seven. Then it finally clicks in my mind who I wrote this to. No way. That's not possible.

My eyes widen as I look up at Zayden, the features finally kicking me in the butt. The green and blue eyes, he had that. The tiny freckle in between his lip and nose, he had that.

But that can't be possible. Does that mean he lied? I can't stop the thought from going through my mind. "Ali?" Zayden calls out to me, seeing my expression. I can't even look at him anymore.

I plaster a fake smile on my face and smile at everyone but Zayden. "Sorry for being so dramatic, it's nothing. Let's just have a fun dinner" it's not just nothing. I kinda feel betrayed.

I'm not so mad about him being who I think he is. I'm madder at the fact he didn't tell me. And lied about it too. God, how could he tell me all those lies with a straight face?

I never had many friends back in Oregon, my ass. Everyone went back to their conversations before but there was still some awkwardness lingering in the air.

Zayden and I didn't speak to each other for the rest of the dinner. Of course, he tried but I ignored him. Yes, it sounds petty but don't you think I have the right to be upset?

I'm not upset to the point where I feel the need to storm away from the table. That's doing too much, I just need some space.

When dinner is over, I carry some of the plates over to the sink and begin to wash them. I can feel someone staring at me so I turn around to meet Zayden's gaze. Of course.

He walks up and sets three more plates into the sink. I side-eye him. Only because I want to catch a glimpse of his expression knowing that I won't speak to him.

Yeah, that's all.

"I'm sorry" he speaks out, leaning against the counter as I rinse a plate. I ignore him. I want to go to my room as fast as possible.

"I just didn't know how to tell you. I was going to tell you but then the more lies I told the harder it got for me to say the truth. And now the lies are eating me in the butt."

Once again, I ignore him. Finally, after rinsing the last plate, I dry my hands and prepare myself for a getaway.

Before I can even get away I feel a hand on my shoulder trying to stop me. Zayden, of course. "Ali, please let me explain." He looks at me with sincere eyes. Like he actually feels sorry. I scoff and push his hand away making my move again.

But yet again, I'm stopped but this time by hands on my waist. Why there out of all places? He turns me around so I'm facing him. "Zayden, let go of me," I tell him, trying to escape out of his grasp. "Ali, please." He begs. There's no point in him trying, if he wants me to talk to him he should give me space first.

"Zayden, if you really want me to talk to you, how about you give me space to clear my mind first?" I calmly say.

He lets out a huge breath before releasing me from his hands. Finally. I retreat to my room with no trouble from anyone.

Falling onto my bed, I stare at the ceiling. A lot of the memories flooded through my head.

And a question flies around my mind. Why?

Why? Why? Why? Why? Why? Why? A million times why. Why lie? Why hide it? Just why.

I won't lie, I'm happy. But disappointed.

I just wish he told me.

❤❤❤❤Authors Note

Okay well yeah! I don't really like when the mc storms away when they're mad. Sometimes it's tolerable but not a lot yk? Guys don't worry Ali forgives him soon but there will be some drama that doesn't really include the fact that he didn't tell her. A totally diff kinda drama. Bear with me okay, I promise they'll kiss soon !

29 | Comfort

Zayden

I hate myself. Why didn't I just tell her? Now she won't talk to me. This morning she walked right past me when I tried talking to her.

She ate a bowl of cereal while staring at her phone the entire time then retreated to her room. She's full-on ignoring me and I can't blame her. I'm not sure if I'd do the same in her position but I certainly would be disappointed.

As I'm staring at the ceiling I hear my phone buzz, meaning I got a text message. I immediately shoot up and grab it from the counter hoping it's from her, but it's not.

It's from an unknown number. I sigh and set my phone down on the bed beside me.

My phone keeps going off and when I finally check it still hoping it's her, I see it's from that unknown number.

Having enough, I open the message to see what it's about and I wish I could go back in time and never open that message.

Unknown

Zayden, it's me your father.I know I've messed up and believe meI regret everything I ever did. I was stupid and couldn't realize how muchyour mom loved me. I'm sorry I missed a huge part of your life. I'm sorry I missed Summers life. But ifyou let me back in your life, I wouldbe so happy. I'm not doing so well right now and I need support. Pleaseget back to me and maybe call me, I want to hear your voice.

Is this a joke? How does this unknown number know me and Summers's names? Before I can process anything, the unknown number calls me. I debate whether I should answer or not.

If it's really my "father" like they say, should I answer? I made the dumbest decision ever by answering.

There was silence for a moment before the person on the other end spoke up. "Zayden?" Shit, it sounds exactly how I remember.

No. No. No. No. No. No. No. Is this a joke?

I swallow the huge spit that gathered up in my mouth. "Jacob?" My "father's" name is Jacob. I know that he's my birth father and that I should call him "Dad" but why should I call someone who hasn't even tried to make contact with me for six years my "dad"?

"Zayden, it's good to hear from you, you're voice has changed a lot." Well no shit, you left me when I was eleven fucking years old. "How did you get this number?" I harshly say, swallowing another lump of spit.

"Let's just say I have my ways" I hear him laugh. So this is funny to him. "So how have you been?" He asks and I hear shuffling from the other end.

Since when does he care? He hasn't cared for the last six years why does he care now? "Great" I don't want to say too many words to him.

"That's good, my son." Son? "I'm not your son, not anymore" I bluntly tell him. I'm not being harsh, I'm being reasonable.

"You are my son, I raised you." Is he serious right now? "Yeah, and you couldn't raise me past the age of eleven" I shoot back having enough of his bullshit.

I can hear him scoff from the other end. "That doesn't change the fact that I am your father!" He raises his voice. Oh, how I wish I could punch the daylights out of him right now.

"Yeah and my stepdad is more fatherly than you ever were." I can hear more shuffling around through the phone before he speaks again. "Wait, your mother remarried?" And of course, he doesn't know anything.

He tries coming back into my life without knowing anything. "Yes and she's happier than ever, so don't you ever try and ruin that, Jacob." Yeah, you will never catch me calling that guy dad again.

"I am your father Zayden, you should address me as your dad." He raises his voice. Yeah and I'm done with him now. "Never again will I call you Dad. Don't talk to me, don't call me, I never want you in my life ever again, goodbye Jacob." I say before hanging up.

Maybe I was too harsh? I mean he was my father after all.

I can feel the bottled-up tears make their way out of my eyes until I'm full-on sobbing. I never cry, I never feel the need to cry. Until last night and today. Oh, and yes, I sobbed a little last night. But we don't mention it.

My small sobs turn to full-on silent crying. There was a knock on my door but I ignored it, I couldn't really see with the tears covering my sight. There was another knock but I just couldn't get up.

The door opens and through my clouded eyes I can make out a face. Ali.

Shit, she's standing in the doorway staring at me. I wipe my eyes and force a smile toward her. But she doesn't say a word.

She closes the door and comes up to me. My tears are probably still visible to her because she wraps her arms around me. "Zayden" she settles herself on the bed, still holding me carefully. "Why are you crying Zayden?"

She's so gentle, even though she was mad earlier. And now I can't contain it, I full-on burst tears in her arms. But she doesn't seem bothered, she just holds me and caresses my back. "Ali, why?" I hold her tightly.

"Why what, Zayden?" Her hands make their way to my hair as she rubs it softly. She repositions us until she's laying down and I'm on top of her, laying on her chest. "Why did he leave us?" I breathe out, letting the tears fall onto her shirt.

"Your dad?" She asks, playing with my hair. I nod. God, I feel so stupid. I never let anyone see me cry, but here I am crying in her arms like a lost little kid. Maybe I still am one?

"I don't know, Zay." She pulls me closer to her and just rubs my back.

She sure knows how to cheer someone up. Even if she just stood there watching me cry, I'd feel some comfort knowing she's there.

I don't want to let go. I hold her tightly, and she doesn't seem bothered. She's holding me while running her hands through my hair. We sit in silence while I sob. I feel better knowing that she's there.

Ali picks up my phone and shows it to me. "Can you unlock your phone please?" I'll just give her the password. "The password is 5673," I tell her and see her eyes widen a little.

"Why'd you tell me the password?" She asks, unlocking my phone. "Because I trust you and I don't have anything to hide from you. Not anymore." That gains a smile from her. It's true, she's the person I trust the most.

I watch as she reads the message from my "father" before blocking the number and deleting it from my phone. She smiles at me before pulling me back into her chest.

And then she does something unexpected. She kisses my head, repeatedly in a calming matter. Fuck, I think I'm getting butterflies.

It really does help with calming me down though, how does she know how to calm me down? Only a few minutes ago I was full-on bursting into tears, now I'm being held like a baby who's getting kisses on the head.

But it's too calming. Because my vision becomes blurry and soon everything is black.

Sleep.

❤❤❤❤Authors Note

AAAAA THIS WAS KINDA FUN TO WRITE. But Zayden my baby I love him so much and ugh. The way Ali calmed him down so easily, I want someone to do that to me. :(anyways u almost got a kiss scene ;) not yet tho but soon.

i promise this slow burn will unslowburn soon believe me !

30 | Christmas Eve

Aliyia

I'm lying in Zayden's bed with him passed out asleep in my arms. I am still a little disappointed that he didn't tell me about our past together but that doesn't matter right now. What matters is him.

I was coming out to the bathroom when I heard Zayden on the phone with someone. I could hear things along the line of "raising past the age of eleven" and Zayden's stepdad.

I knew about Zayden's father not being in their life anymore. I just never knew why. And honestly, I think it's best if I don't know.

Immediately after I heard him hang up the call I pressed myself onto his door and heard him sobbing. I couldn't just stand there and do nothing. I know he would comfort me so why shouldn't I do the same?

Zayden shuffles in my arms and I can tell he's waking up. My hands are still in his hair. It's so fluffy I can't get enough of it. Zayden's eyes flutter open and he lifts his head to look at me, a smile forming on his lips as he stares at my eyes.

"Hi" I greet him. "Hi" he greets back. He slowly gets off me and lays beside me and I suddenly feel empty. The warmth of him in my arms made me feel good, I miss it.

I move so I'm laying on my side, looking at him. He's smiling like a little kid, looking at me. "Aren't you mad at me?" He asks, wiping his chin. That causes me to smile. "I am mad at you." That is a lie.

I stopped being mad a long time ago. I just wanted to see how long I could go without speaking to him. Not a very long time though. His eyes drift from mine for a moment before they reach the again.

"Thank you," he says, his smile increasing. "For what?" I ask even though I know what. "For comforting me, I needed that."

My smile increases as well. His hand suddenly reaches out to push my hair behind my air and I swear I can feel butterflies flying around my stomach. We were so close to each other. My heartbeat increased and it felt like it would plop out of my chest at any moment.

"I can't sleep anymore," he tells me. It's nighttime now, he slept for an hour while I stayed up to make sure nothing happened to him.

"Well I can, I'm gonna go, okay?" I want him to tell me to stay. I don't know why but I want him to. If he told me to then I would. "Can you sleep here tonight?" He asks, his eyes never leaving mine. Thank God.

"Well if you insist" I shrug and close my eyes. I discreetly open my eyes to see him staring at me. Yeah, no way. I turn around so my back is faced to him. "I can't sleep knowing you're staring at me, Zayden."

My heart was beating fast. That earned a chuckle from him. "Goodnight, Ali" he mumbles. I turn my head for a moment to get a glance at him but of course, he's looking right at me. I quickly turn around and try hiding my smile.

"Goodnight, Zayden." My mind is clouded with thoughts for a good ten minutes before I finally drift off to sleep.

My eyes slowly start to open. When I reach full conscientious, I can feel a pair of arms wrapped around my waist. I turn my head and I'm met with Zayden's sleeping figure.

He looks so calm, and safe. His mouth is slightly open and there's a little bit of drool dripping onto the corners of his mouth.

I never knew someone could look so good, even in their sleep. I did not just say that.

I don't want to disturb him while he sleeps so I refrain from getting up. Instead, I reach over to grab my phone from the nightstand.

To my surprise, it's Christmas Eve, meaning tomorrow is Christmas. Not gonna lie, I completely forgot that today was going to be Christmas Eve.

Yesterday I was still a little pissed at Zayden so it never crossed my mind. And also it never crossed my mind when I comforted him because I didn't want to stray from him. My mindset was clear. Everything about last night was all about Zayden. I hated seeing him cry.

That's the first time in like seven years that I've seen him cry. But as a kid, he didn't cry much, only occasionally when he got hurt. But those were mostly sobs. Not full-on crying like last night. My heart still aches for him, seeing him break down in my arms made all the "anger" I felt in me fly away.

Suddenly, the arms snaked around my waist tighten the hold on me and a head comes nuzzling against the back of my neck. Zayden.

I'm sure he's half awake right now. Now that I think about it, this is the second time we've slept in the same bed and the morning outcome was the same both times.

I would wake up to Zayden's arms around my waist. And for some odd reason, I didn't mind it. To be completely honest, I felt safe in his arms. The same way he felt safe in mine last night.

I think Zayden and I have some type of unbreakable bond that's kept us together all these years. Well, maybe not all these years. But throughout the time we've been together.

Zayden shuffles a little from behind me as he holds me closer to him. "Ali," he says with his amazingly attractive morning voice.

I smile at his words and respond quickly. "Morning, Zayden," I turn to face him to see his eyes fully open, looking back at me.

He shoots me a weak smile. "Morning, Ali." Why, just why does someone's morning voice have to be so attractive?

Wanting to feel more comfortable, I turn my entire body to face him. Once again, we're very close to each other.

Is it bad that I kinda want him to kiss me?

I mean I've never had my first kiss but I'm gonna be seventeen in a couple of months and I still haven't had my first kiss. Nor have I ever done anything with anyone, like been in a relationship.

My life is sad, to be honest. Well not sad, I would say boring. So even if it is my first kiss, I wouldn't mind kissing Zayden.

"How'd you sleep?" I ask him, not daring to look away from our little staring contest. He shrugs a little and his smile fades. "Good, you?" By the looks of it, it doesn't sound good.

"My sleep was okay, thank you for asking" I smile at him until he finally cracks and looks away. I mentally cheer myself on. Winner, as always.

That's a joke.

"Are you sure you slept well?" I ask him, trying to get his eyes to meet mine again. "You sounded a little off when I asked,"

Zayden's eyes finally meet mine again and a smile plasters on his face like all the emotion was just wiped off of him. "I promise I slept well, you don't have to worry but thank you for asking."

I know this isn't the time but his morning voice, gosh. Who knows, maybe one of these days I'll end up being whipped for him.

I highly doubt it though, he's the whipped one. He has always been whipped. Even in the first grade. Zayden's supposed to be a senior in high school right now but he's a junior because he started school later than he was supposed to.

But as I was saying, when we first became friends in the first grade, he gave me half of his lunch when I finished my entire lunch during snack time. What can I say, I was practically starving.

And throughout the days, he kept sharing his lunches with me and that's how we became best friends.

Shaking my head to clear my thoughts, I realize I was zoned out staring at Zayden. Oops.

"I should go to my room now," I try getting up but Zayden puts his hands on my waist, stopping me from doing so. "No, please stay" I look at him with confusion written all over my face but I don't protest.

I nod and lay back down beside him. We just sit in comfortable silence for a bit before he speaks out. "Do you wanna watch a movie?" Um, yes! I love movies with my whole heart.

"Yeah, what movie?" I hope it's Christmas-themed. "Not sure but I'm thinking Christmas themed?" Did he just read my mind? There's no way.

I think for a moment until the lightbulb in my head shines. "Elf?" It's one of the best Christmas movies, you can't say I'm wrong. Zayden smiles at me and gestures at the remote on the nightstand. "Elf sounds good."

Why did a thousand butterflies just start flying around my stomach? I reach over to grab the remote and toss it to him. And like the show off he is, he catches it with one hand.

Wow very impressive.

"Oh yeah, Ali?" He calls out to me. I look at him and make a humming sound.

"Merry Christmas Eve."

❤❤❤❤Authors Note

This chapter is longer than I intended it to be, sorry about that. I love them so much they are my babies. Also is it "happy Christmas Eve" or "merry Christmas Eve?" LMAO IDK THE DIFFERENCE

31 | Onesies

Zayden

God, everything about Ali is so perfect. I can't stop thinking about how she held me in her arms last night. I can't stop thinking about how she kissed my head and held me till I fell asleep.

Emphasis on the kissing my head part.

She left my room a while ago after we watched Elf. When she left my room I felt empty. Not a depressing empty but an empty where I missed her touch.

I wish what happened last night could happen every night. Without the crying, of course, just the part where she held me close. And did I mention her kissing my head?

There's a knock on my door and I jolt up in excitement, hoping it's who I see it is. When I open the door I see Lukas standing there with an idiotic grin on his face.

I look at his grinning face with confusion. "What's up?" I dab him up.

Boy greetings.

"Remember those unicorn and Pikachu onesies we bought a while back ago?" He asks, letting himself into my room and plopping down on the bed.

Lukas and I bought two unicorn onesies and two Pikachu onesies a few days before our flight to Hawaii. The girls don't know about it, we wanted to surprise them with onesies but I never thought it would be this soon.

"Yeah? What about them?" I plop down beside him. "Why don't we give it to the girls tonight? That way we can all wear them tomorrow while we open presents and all that." Lukas says, his eyes scanning my room a little.

Hmm, sounds like a plan. "Alright but how exactly are we going to pick who gets which onesie?" I ask him.

The grin on his face expands. "We don't. I'm gonna take the unicorn ones with my girlfriend and you can take the Pikachu ones with Aliyia. That way we can match with our girls."

I almost choke on my spit when he referred to the girls as our girls. Aka, Tate being his girl, and Ali... being my girl.

Won't lie, I immediately started picturing Ali in both the unicorn and Pikachu onesie. And from what my imagination created, the Pikachu one fits her perfectly.

I pretend to think it over for a moment even though I wanted to scream out a yes. "Okay, we can do that," I tell him, seeing the smug look on his face. "We should do something like now. We haven't done much and we're in fucking Hawaii."

"Yeah, but Hawaii is probably another vacation to you considering you come here like every year and own a beach house." He's right. Don't want to sound spoilt or anything but it's true.

Hawaii was just another vacation to me. But I'm proud of it. Because all thanks to my mom we have this opportunity to come here every year. No thanks to that idiot who calls himself my father.

"Since we're going out, why not go out in our onesies? How cool would that be? Walking around where Pikachu and unicorn onesies in Hawaii! That could be a once-in-a-lifetime chance." Lukas tells me.

"Uh huh, anyways let's go out, inform the girls" Lukas scrunches up his nose when I say the word "inform" but doesn't say anything about it and simply nods.

Lukas gets up and makes a break for the door before stopping and turning to me, the smug grin on his face again. "I'll get Tate, you get Aliyia."

Before I can say anything he's already shutting the door. He did that on purpose. He doesn't even have the onesies, I have them.

Heading for my closet, I dig through it looking for the onesies. When I find them, I take out the Pikachu ones and exit my room.

I knock on Ali's door which is directly from mine. Before she opens the door I clear my throat and run my hands through my hair, trying to make it look good.

Her door opens and I'm met with her in a different pair of clothes. She slightly smiles when she sees me but it's immediately replaced with a look of confusion.

Her eyes avert to the curled-up yellow onesies in my hand before fixating her gaze on me. "Hi."

"Hi," I say back, gripping the onesies tightly. Why am I getting so nervous around her? "Is something wrong?" She asks, her eyes filled with concern.

Not one bit. "No, I just have a" I pause. "Surprise." I wasn't sure if I should call it a surprise or not because it's not super interesting, but it's alright.

Her face lights up a little and I can see the corner of her lips curve for one moment before they're replaced with a look of confusion. "Oh yeah?" She tits her head. "What is it?"

I grin before pulling the onesies from behind my back into her view. And I swear to you, her eyes lit up brighter than a damn candle. But once again, every emotion on her face was wiped away and I received an impressed but not so impressed look. Quite disappointing, I was kinda excited about these onesies.

"Wow" is all she lets out as she stares at the two pieces of yellow fabric in my hand.

Just gonna ignore the fact that I was hoping she'd jump in my arms all excited with that gleaming face I miss so much. Is it bad that I want to kiss her? Of course, that's bad.

Is it?

Maybe.

My grin leaves my face as I just stand awkwardly in front of her room holding two yellow pieces of fabric. Clearing my throat, I finally grow the balls to say something. "Uh, we're going out, if you want to come" I hold up the onesies higher. "Wearing these."

Sounds embarrassing, I know. But when you're with the right group of friends you shouldn't have a care in the world.

And then she does it. She lets out the smile that I've missed so dearly. Maybe not her usual smile and this one seems just a tiny bit forced but I can sense a genuine part. "Sounds embarrassing but also sounds like fun."

"Definitely embarrassing," I tell her, allowing my smile to return to my face. Her green eyes that are the shade of Mountain Dew look from my eyes, to the onesies, then back to my eyes.

I really want to kiss her.

But I know she hasn't had her first kiss yet, and I want it to be with someone special to her.

"So which one is mine?" She asks, keeping the smile planted on her face, making sure it doesn't stray. I hand her the one in my right hand which is a little bit smaller than the one in my left.

She hangs it above her head and examines it. "Pretty nice if you ask me." You're pretty nice if you ask me. Wait does that even make sense?

Lord, why am I saying things like this?

It's weird.

All my mind can think about right now is her lips on mine, my hands on her waist, and hers in my hair. Having the best kiss of our lives.

Not the best thing to think about.

I'm standing there gawking at her like a fool. She notices my staring and shifts slightly in discomfort. Shit, did I stare too long? "Sorry" I whisper.

But she just smiles at me. "I'll be ready in twenty," she says before stepping back and lightly shutting the door in my face.

God, why am I so awkward and nervous? No, I'm only awkward and nervous around her. She makes me this way.

Why is that?

❤❤❤❤Authors Note

I might start rushing the chapters a little bc I'm the author but I still don't like the fact that im haven't made them kiss yet and we are on chapter 30. I feel sorry for you guys so that's why I have a surprise coming yk *smooch smooch*

32 | Escape Place

A liyia

I hold the onesie close to me as I bite back a smile. I don't know why but I really wanted to jump into his arms and smile at him.

But it didn't want to come out.

And for some odd reason, I felt the urge to kiss him. Strange huh?

Once I hear his bedroom door close I start jumping and squealing like how a little kid would react when their parents gave them candy. That type of squealing.

Why am I squealing? Gosh if I knew.

But sue me for loving the way his eyes look at me. Sue me for wanting him to stare at me longer than he did. Sue me for just wanting to kiss him and hold him again. Sue me.

Setting the onesie down on my bed, I look in the mirror to see red cheeks. I hope he didn't see that.

I've spent five out of twenty minutes of my time thinking about Zayden, leaving me only fifteen minutes to get ready. Luckily, I had already taken a shower so all there is left is to get in my onesie and do some makeup.

I don't know what's going on in their heads though. Wearing a damn heavy onesie in this weather? It's gonna be melting today. We're all gonna melt like ice cubes.

After fitting into the Pikachu onesie which surprisingly fit very well, I apply some mascara and lipgloss to my face.

I know I said makeup but I'm not really feeling it. I've been going natural recently and honestly, I think it fits me better.

Tate bursts into my room, not even knocking. She's wearing a white unicorn onesie that also fits her perfectly. Why did I think we were all wearing the same onesies?

Not long after, the boys fill in the room. Ever heard of knocking? I notice that Tate and Lukas are matching which leaves me and Zayden matching.

He looks amazing in that onesie though.

Not that I care though.

"Do you guys know how to knock?" I cross my arms, staring at the three of them. "Nope!" Lukas grins. That bastard.

Sighing, I grab my phone from my bed and make my way to them but Tate puts her pointer finger up like she just got an idea. "Group picture, now!" She demands, taking my phone from my hand and going to the camera app.

Didn't even wait for my response but okay. She sets up the camera which is set to take pictures every three seconds.

I pose beside her while the boys just stand there, not posing. I turn to look at them, ignoring the fact that my phone is taking pictures.

"Come on boys, pose." They both look at me at the same time before Zayden hops on Lukas's back.

Not what I was expecting at all but I'll allow it.

We continue taking pictures for a while before we finally decide it's time to start going. Come to think of it, where are we even going?

"Guys, where are we going?" I ask, placing my phone in the small pocket of my onesie. Zayden smiles at me before responding. "We are picking a Christmas tree." isn't that supposed to be done days before Christmas and not on Christmas Eve?

I don't say anything other than letting out a small "o".

I groan. "Why are all these trees so ugly?" Lukas turns to face me and scoffs. "The trees aren't ugly, you're just picky." He's mad that we didn't get the tree he liked.

Can you blame us? It was horrendous. Not really tall, skinny, and missing many branches. "Oh please, you're just mad we didn't get the ugly skinny tree, Lukas" I shoot back. It's true.

Before he can say anything more, he's interrupted by the voice I love so much. "What about this one?" Zayden points to the most perfect tree I've ever laid my eyes on.

It was tall enough to fit in the house, in between slim and thick, and it had just enough leaves and branches to make it look full. "Holy fuck" Tate and I let out at the same time.

"I think this is the one" Tate says, approaching the tree. Lukas just stands there, examining the tree. "I don't get what's so good about it. My tree was better," he won't let that go huh?

"We have to get this one!" I exclaim, holding myself back from jumping onto Zayden and pressing a million kisses on his forehead, thanking him for finding my dream tree.

Why am I getting so excited? It's a damn tree, Aliyia, a tree.

"Alright, we're getting this one," Zayden announces to one of the workers nearby.

A whole process goes by and Zayden ends up paying for the whole thing. This guy doesn't even have a job where does he get this money from? Oh right, he's a mommy's boy.

That's hot.

No, it's not.

Yes, it is.

"It's really bothering how this leaf is poking at my sides" Tate squirms in the backseat, the middle seat down and in between Tate and Lukas who I'm sure would do anything to cuddle right now.

I try to contain my laughter because I know if I was in her position I would be uncomfortable too. Good thing I'm not.

Our families were impressed by the perfect tree we picked and everyone instantly started decorating it. Adding family ornaments, decorative lights, and anything to make the tree ten times better.

They even surprised us with Christmas Eve dinner to thank us for the dinner we prepared for them during their arrival and for the tree.

It's now eleven on the dot and I can't sleep. No matter how hard I close my eyes, I just can't, it's tiring.

I groan as I flip my pillow around to the colder side, hoping it would help me sleep. Which it did not.

I have the sudden urge to go to Zayden's room. I try to call it off for a few seconds but my body betrays me and makes its way out of my room, into the hall, and knocks on Zayden's door.

When he doesn't open the door after a few seconds, I get the hint that he's asleep and turn to go to my room when the door finally opens.

I'm met with a half awake, messy hair, Pikachu onesie wearing Zayden. "Sorry did I wake you up?" I apologize, feeling a mount of guilt flow through me. He rubs his eyes and softly smiles at me.

"No you didn't wake me up, I couldn't sleep." He mumbles with a sleepy voice that is way too much for me to handle now. Something inside me is telling me he's lying but I choose to stupidly ignore it.

"Is everything okay, Ali?" He asks, worries plastered on his face now. "No I just couldn't sleep either and I was bored." Very bored but I don't add the extra unneeded details.

He simply smiles and leans against his doorway. The way that the hood of his Pikachu onesie is dragged over the top of his head, and the-

"Ali! Did you hear me?" Shit, I must've zoned out. "Sorry what?" He tilts his head, his eyes studying me. "I said do you want to get out of here and do something fun."

Depends on the fun. "What type of fun?" I question and immediately regret it after I see the smirk on his face. He better not mean anything inappropriate because that's a big no-no from me.

Instead of responding he just shuts his door and interlocks his fingers with mine. Holy. Fucking. Shit.

He leads me down the stairs and gestures for me to put shoes on. I slip on my Air Force 1s and follow him out the back of the house. "You gonna tell me where we're going?" I ask, trailing directly behind him, my hand still interlocked with his.

"Let's just say" he starts. "My escape place." Sounds interesting my life-threatening. What if he's planning to kill me? "You're not going to brutally murder me right?" I need confirmation.

He lets out a laugh, picking up his pace. "No, I'm not going to brutally murder you, Ali," suspicious.

A few minutes after walking, we reach what seems to be an empty park. "A park is your escape place?" I question. He nods. "Mainly at night though, where it's quiet." He leads me to the swings and sets himself down on one.

I sit on the swing directly beside me and lightly start swinging myself. I look up at the moon and stars in the sky, they shine bright.

"It's really pretty you know" I let out. Zayden fixates his gaze on me. "Huh?" Oops, didn't make that clear. "The sky, the moon, perhaps the stars. It's all so pretty. Sometimes I wish I could be like them."

"Do you mean like, be pretty?" He questions, slightly swinging himself as well. I nod and look at him. "I think you're prettier than all three combined." He mumbles and I can just barely make out what he said but when I do I turn away from him to hide the look on my face.

"Shit, did I say that out loud," he asks and I can hear the embarrassment in his voice. I nod, still facing away from him.

After some awkward silence, we engage in conversation for what felt like hours but was actually only twenty minutes. "I think we should head back now," I tell him, getting off the swing.

He nods in agreement and copies my movement. The urge to kiss him suddenly grows stronger and I have a feeling he can sense it too because while we're waking, he grabs my wrist and makes me turn around to face him.

"Ali," he says, his hands tightening on my wrist, but not in a painful way. "Is it bad that I really want to kiss you right now?"

Not at all. "Maybe a little." What a fucking lie. I would be so happy if he kissed me.

"And what would you do if I did start kissing you?" He asks, grabbing my other wrist and pulling me towards him. That's when I feel drops of rain on me.

Little spits, then full-on rain in a matter of fifteen seconds. "I don't know what I would do." Yes, I do, I would kiss him back. Even though I don't know how to and definitely don't know how to do it well, I'd still do it.

I feel him move closer to me, and surprisingly I don't move away. I don't feel anything other than rain falling down my face.

That is until his face is an inch from mine and I can hear his heavy breathing. "You sure, Ali?" He reassures, cupping my cheek. I nod, making sure it's not too eagerly. I want him to kiss me right fucking now.

And with that, he moves his face even closer to mine. And that's when I feel it. A feeling I've been waiting for, for sixteen years.

His lips on mine.

❤❤❤❤Authors Note

FUCKING FINALLY LETS GO THEY KISSSRD WHOOP WHOPP! AND IN THE RAIN?? ISNT THAT THE BEST FIRST KISD PLACE IM SO JEALOUS BRO

the onesies

33 | Merry Christmas

Aliyia

Zayden fucking Gryant, my best friend since childhood is kissing me right now. And I'm standing in shock as if I didn't see it coming. And also because I have no damn clue how to fucking kiss someone back.

He pulls away from my lips, his hand remaining on my cheek, and frowns. "I'm sorry, did you not want that?" Oh God, I did want that.

I shake my head and avoid eye contact. "No, I do it's just" I stare at the cement below me. Zayden hums and I can tell he's staring at me. "Of course, I want this you idiot, I just don't know how to kiss someone back." It sounds so embarrassing I know, but exactly how do I do it? I need written instructions and a demonstration.

Zayden just smirks at me. "That's okay, ill teach you. Just follow my lips," I have a feeling I'll mess that up too but I just nod and lean into the kiss.

I can feel the raindrops on my face when I meet Zayden's lips again. The hand on my cheek was cold from the rain.

And just like that, I'm kissing Zayden. I do exactly what he told me to do and followed his lip movements. I'm sure I messed it up at the start but eventually, I got the hang of it. It's not so hard. Why have I never kissed anybody in my life?

Zayden's hands traveled to my waist while mine reached out to wrap around his neck. Is it bad for friends to kiss like this? Probably not.

It's just all in the moment that's all.

Yeah.

After what felt like the best hours of my life, Zayden pulls away from my lips, his hand remaining on my waist. "Wow." He blurts, a smile creeping onto his face. "Sorry if that wasn't good," I apologize, avoiding his expression.

"Wow," he says again. When I look up at him his eyes are lit up, and he looks happy, shocked, and amazed all in one.

I tilt my head in confusion, my arms retreating from his neck. "That was fucking amazing, Ali. Who taught you how to kiss like that?"

You.

I shrug. "Well, I did follow your lead as you told me to." His arms retreat from my waist and are tucked into the pocket of the onesie. That stupid smirk that makes me feel things in my stomach returns to his face.

"Well, shall we head back?" He checks his phone and his smirk widens. "Can you believe it, Ali? We kissed all the way to Christmas."

Holy shit.

My eyes widen. "Wait what?" He nods. "Yup, I assumed it turned twelve o clock in the middle of our kiss," stupid smirk.

Well, that's shocking. I put on my hood to cover my hair from the pouring rain. Zayden begins to walk away and signals for me to follow him.

"So, did you enjoy your first kiss?" I can practically hear the smirk on his voice. My cheeks get heated and I look down to avoid him seeing the red that's probably on my face. "Mhm," I hum.

"What was that? Use your words, Ali" He's doing this on purpose. "Yes, I enjoyed it Zayden." This is so embarrassing.

I hear him hum in response and seconds later he wraps one arm around my waist while we continue to walk back to the beach house.

Butterflies are flapping around my stomach right now. That was so unexpected but I don't mind. It totally doesn't make me want to scream into my pillow later.

"Are you liking your stay in Hawaii?" He asks, completely changing the subject. I nod. "Yeah it's really beautiful here, you're lucky you get to come here like every year." I look up at him to see him smiling at me.

"I mean, you could always come with us again next year" he squeezes my waist softly. "I'll think about it" yeah right, I've made up my mind already. Who would turn down going to Hawaii almost every year?

I hear Zayden sigh. "Ali."

"Yeah?" What's up with him? "I-" he starts and stops himself before he can say anything else. Huh? Weird. "Yeah?" I say again, this time with a slightly demanding voice. "Uh, I was just gonna say we should stop by the beach, it's on our way anyways."

Something inside me is telling me he's lying but I ignore it because going to the beach in the middle of the night has always been one of my dreams.

"That would be fun," I tell him, trying to hide the smile that's fighting to crawl up my face. Fucking smiles. Zayden simply smiles and changes our course of direction to the beach.

Being at the beach at night felt like a fever dream. Thirteen-year-old me would scream with joy right now.

Zayden and I are walking along the sandy beach, the waves forming beside us. His hands left from my waist a while ago when we arrived. Not that I wanted them to stay there anyways.

I look up at him to catch him already looking at me with that idiot smile of his. Why does he always look at me like that? I don't cave in though, I hold my eyes on him until he finally looks away and clears his throat.

I bite back a laugh and look at the waves trying to reach my feet. "The beach at night is really beautiful" I hear Zayden say. He's right, it feels so unreal to be here right now. While everyone else was probably asleep considering it's Christmas morning.

"Yeah, it is" I agree, looking at Zayden whose eyes were fixated on the waves and not me for once. Too bad, I like when he stares at me.

What the fuck? No, I don't.

Just before I get the chance to look away, his eyes meet mine and I feel a knot in my stomach. And he flashes his teeth at me. Stupid grin.

Zayden tilts his head and pokes his inner cheek with his tongue. "You just like staring at me huh, Ali," he's one to talk.

"No, I don't" I defend myself. I always catch him staring so he can't talk right now.

He hind. "Yeah you do, you know you just take a picture, it lasts longer"

I cringe at his words. "You're annoying," he got on my nerves a lot. "Yeah but you like it, don't you Ali?" I almost fell to my knees because of the way he said that.

Yes, I really do like it.

No, I don't, what the fuck?

When I don't say anything, Zayden takes it as his cue to laugh. Fucking weirdo. "You're so corny Zayden," I tell him, still cringing from his words earlier. And before he can say anything I stop him by putting my hand to his face. "And don't you dare say some corny shit right now, I'll punch you in the throat."

From the corner of my eye, I can see a slight smirk on his face. Fucking weirdo.

"Yes ma'am," he said, tucking his hands in his onesie pocket.

Holy shit on a stick.

After spending almost an hour walking alongside the waves and talking, we call it a day. Or night? And head back to the beach house.

Before I can enter my room he speaks. "Merry Christmas Ali, see you later" and with that, he retreats to his room before I can get a word in. Holy shit on a stick.

Yeah, I could barely sleep that night. All I could think about was the amazing kiss in the rain with him.

Best fucking kiss ever.

34 | Come With Me

Zayden

I'd be lying if I said I didn't spend half of my night thinking about that kiss. Like I could barely sleep, my mind just kept replaying that moment.

I'd also be lying if I said I didn't enjoy that kiss. That's the best kiss I've ever had and I've technically only had one with someone else. Someone who is not relevant to me anymore. Not that she ever was.

Just when I felt the slightest bit sleepy, my mom bursts into my room with a happy smile on her face. "Merry Christmas, my dear!" She practically shouts.

I try hiding how tired I am right now with a smile. "Merry Christmas, mom," I smile at her. "Get up, everyone's downstairs already," she says, the smile not leaving her face.

Christmas is my mother's favourite holiday. She gets overly excited about it every year. She's not even that fond of the gift aspect, mainly the time she spends with us. Christmas is one of the only days of the year that we spend the entire day with our mom.

Of course there is some over the year but with my hockey it's become difficult for the whole family to spend it together.

"Okay, I'll be down in a bit let me freshen up," I force myself out of the bed and make my way to the bathroom, shutting the door. I hear her say something along the lines of not taking too long.

I stare at myself in the mirror, admiring the pikachu onesie and the memories from last night. God, something is seriously wrong with me.

I shake away the thoughts and start washing my face. And as soon as my eyes shut close, I'm met with Ali standing in her pikachu onesie. Quickly drying my face I open my eyes and Ali isn't there. Holy, fuck, shit, am I hallucinating?

"Zayden!" I hear my mom yell from downstairs. Shit, I completely forgot I had to be downstairs. Rushing out of the bathroom, I grab my phone from my bed and head out of my room.

When I reach the main floor I see everyone seated on the couch, and some on the floor. Isn't this embarrassing?

My eyes meet Ali's who's seated beside Tate on the couch. I shoot her a smile and she looks away from me.

Uh oh?

I make my way to sit on the ground with Lukas and we do a bro handshake thing before someone speaks up. "When can we open presents?" My sister asks, her eyes focused on the packed presents under the tree.

"Patience, Summer" I tell her, rolling my eyes.

"Well we were planning on going to the beach first then open presents when we get back" My mom speaks up, breaking the silence.

That's actually a decent idea. Decent.

"Sounds good to me" Ali's dad says, wrapping his arms around his wife. Everyone agrees and we all break to our rooms to change.

Soon after, we all meet downstairs again. Preparing to walk down to the beach. I approach Ali who's putting on a pair of Nike Blazers, she's clearly having a hard time with that. Those shoes are no joke.

"Hi," I greet, watching her stand up after tying her shoe. "Hi," she says back, avoiding eye contact. I slightly drown at the fact she's somewhat avoiding me.

Is it because of the kiss we shared last night?

"Is something wrong?" I ask, lowering my voice so only we can hear. She nods and hums but still doesn't look at me. When she tries walking away I grab her wrist, "Ali, talk to me please."

She sighs and finally meets my eyes, those green eyes filled with emotion. "There's nothing wrong Zayden, drop it." She releases herself from my grip and walks to Tate.

Holy fuck, what did I do? I shouldn't have kissed her.

I run my hands through my hair in frustration, I tend to do that a lot. Lukas approaches me and I can see the amusement in his face. "Bro, Zayden what'd you do?" I wish I knew.

I shrug and turn to look at Ali who's talking to Tate about whatever girls talk about.

"Where'd you two disappear off to last night?" Lukas asks, the amusement never leaving his tone. Shit, we're caught. Lukas catches onto my shocked expression and lets out a laugh. "Don't think I didnt notice, Zayden."

"Fuck off" I cover my nervousness with a small laugh. I doubt Ali has told anyone about the kiss so it shouldn't be fair if I tell someone about it.

Ali glances at me but immediately averts her attention to her mother who approaches her. They talk and I can see a small smile crawl up on Ali's face. But it's not genuine.

What the fuck happened?

Less than five minutes later, everyone is walking along the sand towards the beach. I take this as my perfect chance to talk to Ali once more.

"Hi," I say as I approach her. She doesn't look at me but I know she's side eyeing me. "Hi" she mumbles quietly.

We walk in awkward silence for a moment before I finally spoke up. "Is everything okay?" And of course, she doesn't give me a full answer instead she nods. "Ali, you can talk to me you know that right?"

And once again she nods. "Please just give me an answer, Ali."

"What do you want me to say Zayden? I've already told you that nothing is wrong, please just drop it,"She finally speaks, raising her voice slightly but only loud enough for the two of us to here.

"Is it because I kissed you last night?" I question, looking at her face. She scrunches up her face but not in annoyance or anything, pain. "Ali what's wrong?" I ask in a more demanding tone this time.

She stops in her tracks and only then do I notice we are far behind everyone else. "I'm telling you Zayden, it's not that big of a deal I've been through this for years and I just get moody on those days."

I tilt my head in confusing not getting her point. She sighs and continues walking. "It's just a period." She says in a more quiet hushed tone.

Shit.

Stupidity washes all over me. And I can barely even let a word out other than a hushed "oh". I feel so stupid, I shouldn't have begged her to tell me something she didn't feel comfortable with.

"Sorry," I apologize, feeling very dumb right now. She hums and starts walking faster.

And suddenly, I have the best most smartest idea ever. "Wait Ali, I have an idea." She doesn't stop walking but she slows down her pace and looks at me over her shoulder. "Why don't we just stop by at one of those connivence stores nearby?

Ali looks at me confused, one eyebrow raising. "Why?"

I shrug. "Why not? I want to get you something to make you feel better I guess," I see a tiny smile try to crawl out but is immediately replaced with a thin line.

"Don't worry about it Zayden, it's all good" she continues walking at her regular pace, speeding up. I grab her wrist, stopping her in her tracks and once again she gives me a confused look mixed with a "what the fuck are you doing," look.

I shoot her a smile and loosen my grip on her wrist. "Come on Ali. I'll buy you something, anything you want, just please come with me," I look at her with pleading eyes.

I notice that she winces but tries to cover up. She looks over her shoulders where the others are just barely in sight, having already reached the beach. "What about the others? Won't they wonder where we went?" She asks, turning her head back to face me.

"Oh well," I shrug, letting go of her wrist but standing unreasonably close to her.

Not to be weird or anything, I just like her presence. I like being around her. I like her smiles, her hugs, her laughs, her voice, her kisses, and especially her hugs.

Her hugs make me feel so warm and comfortable. I wouldn't mind being trapped in her arms forever.

She thinks it over for a moment before silently agreeing. "We have to be quick though," she adds, turning her course of direction.

Fuck yeah.

🖤🖤🖤🖤Authors Note

sorry i haven't been that active i actually got in 10 car crashes and got arrested and all that so im actually in jail rn i hid my phone so it's all good

35 | Messed Up

A liyia
   I wasn't sure what was with the random kind gesture but honestly, I don't mind it.

I started my period last night when Zayden and I snuck out and I didn't even realize until I woke up this morning. My Pikachu onesie was stained so much and it leaked through onto my bed. I actually wanted to cry.

After all that I simply became moody. Can you blame me? Periods fucking suck ass.

"Sooo," I hear Zayden say from beside me, our bodies inches apart as we walk. "Sooo," I repeat.

I don't have to look at him to know he's already smiling. He does that a lot recently and I love it.

Suddenly a sharp pain shoots me in my lower abdomen, causing me to wince a little. Zayden takes notice of that and grabs my hand, squeezing it reassuringly.

"Um," he clears his throat. "I don't necessarily know how much pain you're feeling right now, but if I could fix it I promise I would."

That was almost cute.

Almost.

I give him a side eye and reply sarcastically. "Thanks, appreciate it," Zayden chuckles a little. "Anytime, Ali."

As we enter the convenience store, I try not to make a run for the ice cream section. I've been craving ice cream all day, especially on a hot day like today.

Zayden makes his way to the candy section with me following behind. He stands in front of the candy and eyes it like he's thinking carefully before turning to me. "See anything you want?"

I scan the candy and sour straps immediately catch my eye. "Those," I point to the sour candy.

Zayden picks up two packages of candy instead of one. "Anything else?" He asks, holding both candies in one hand.

I scan the candy once again and the only thing that catches my eyes are sour patches. There's something about sour candies.

Once again, Zayden picks up two of the packaged sour patches and holds them in his other free hand. "Why so much sweet things?"

I give him a "really?" look because that was a stupid question. We are standing in front of a sugar-filled aisle, what did he expect?

He laughs. "Yeah, yeah, I know." Good.

"Anything else you want here?" He asks, beginning to walk to the cashier. I shake my head and follow him to the cashier.

Shit my ice cream.

Before I can say anything Zayden already handed the cashier a ten-dollar bill. Fuck.

He takes the plastic bag and gestures for me to walk with him.

My ice cream though.

Zayden examines my face for a moment before speaking out. "Something wrong, Ali? You look devastated."

I am. My ice cream.

I shake my head and reach my hand into the bag to grab something. When my hand retreats from the bag I see I picked out the sour straps. This can make up for the ice cream for a while.

Opening the package, I take one sour strap and plop it into my mouth. The sweetness and sourness hit me all at once.

"Can I have one of those?" Zayden asks, eyeing my straps. I shake my head again. "No, you bought two, eat the other one."

He sighs. "I bought both of them for you, so can you please just put one in my mouth," he stops walking and faces me, bending down a little to reach my height and opens his mouth wide.

What. The. Actual. Fuck.

He doesn't budge and just waits there with his mouth wide open. At this point people walking by are giving us glances, better to get this over with.

Sighing, I take one of the sour straps and place it in his mouth, quickly retreating my hand. He chews on it for a moment before he brings out a big smile. "Thanks."

"You're so fucking weird, Zayden. Why would you ask me to do that in public?"

He continues walking and I see a smirk crawl onto his face. "Oh what, you'd rather me ask you in private?"

I turn my head to avoid his face. "Yeah, saves the embarrassment," I hear him laugh from beside me. "Whatever you say, Ali."

I would never admit it out loud but the gesture was somewhat cute. Him asking me to practically feed him sour straps. But I was not lying about the embarrassment. It could've been cute if it wasn't in public.

Could've.

Plus, that's a whole seventeen-year-old with a free hand who could grab it himself. Fucking weirdo.

"You should seriously shut up, Zayden," I tell him, making eye contact with him.

He looks into my eyes for a moment before his smile reaches his eyes, a tiny dimple appearing on his right cheek. "Yes ma'am."

Holy fuck.

We continue walking toward the beach. Well, that's where I thought we were going. I followed Zayden the whole time without even asking if we were returning to the beach.

We should've arrived at the beach by now but I notice ahead of us is the park where we... Yeah.

"Zayden why aren't we heading back to the beach? I thought we were just getting snacks and returning?" I ask, curious about why we're approaching the place we shared a kiss or two last night.

Zayden shrugged, making a beeline for the swings. "Why not I guess? The beach seems boring."

I cross my arms, the empty sour straps package in my hand crackling at the movement. "And so? What if I wanted to go back to the beach?"

Zayden tilts his head, settling himself on the swings and gripping onto the sides. "Well do you?"

No.

"Yes," I face the ground, not wanting him to see that I'm lying.

"Ali, I've known you for a good amount of years to know when your lying or not." He starts. "No need to lie to me."

What makes him think I'm lying?

"What if I'm not lying?" I shoot back, making eye contact to try and prove something but immediately failing when I see his eyes.

Those fucking eyes.

The green eye is on the left and the blue eye is on the right. I'm jealous of his eyes.

Zayden pats the swing beside him, gesturing for me to sit. I wait a good five seconds before sitting down on the swing beside him.

"Can I ask you a question, Ali?" Zayden asks, looking at me with sincere eyes. I have a good feeling I know what that question will be. I nod, trying to be discreet about knowing.

"Are you just going to pretend that what happened last night didn't happen?" There it is.

I knew it.

I sigh, mentally preparing my words carefully. "I don't know what to say about it, Zayden. We kissed, there's not much to it, it was just a kiss," I probably should've worded that better.

"Just a kiss? Is that all it was to you?" I can hear the emotion in his voice. And of course, that wasn't all it was to me. I thought about it all night and morning. But I've never dealt with this sort of stuff.

When I don't answer, Zayden talks again. "Because if that was all it meant to you then I feel stupid for thinking about it all fucking day."

Wait, he thought about it as well?

"What do you mean?"

Zayden scoffs. "What do I mean? I mean I thought about kissing you ever since I laid eyes on you when you moved here. When I found out you were my childhood best friend, something inside me lit up." he sighs.

"You somehow just lit up my days every time I was around you, I wanted to be around you all the time. And when I finally gave in and kissed you last night after holding myself back I thought maybe you felt something for me too. Guess it was just a kiss." he continued.

Holy fuck.

Did he just confess to me? Does he feel something for me? What does he feel? Did I light up his days? He's thought about kissing me for over a month now? My brain cannot process this.

"Zayden-" I try to say something but get cut off by him.

"Don't worry Aliyia, you don't have to explain anything to me. I think it's best we just head back to the beach right now."

Uh oh, he hasn't called me "Aliyia" in a long time.

I messed up.

36 | Gifts

Zayden

Why the fuck did I tell her all that? I didn't mean to say anything like that, especially her name instead of her nickname. It just slipped.

If she doesn't feel the same I shouldn't force it on her.

She's currently walking a few feet behind me, staring at the ground. I should apologize.

But I don't.

The words don't come out.

Why can't I say anything? Just two words are all I need. The "I'm" and the "sorry."

The beach comes into vision and I can see figures huddled up in one area, probably our families. How much time did we even spend gone?

"Zayden can we talk?" I hear a voice from behind me say. I do want to talk, but I'm not in the mood. It's my fault after all, but I still want some space. I shouldn't have rambled like that.

"Aliyia, it's okay you don't have to say anything," I tell her, facing her but not making eye contact. If I looked into her eyes right now I just know I would give in.

"But-" I cut her off, "We can deal with this another time, let's just enjoy Christmas with our families."

She sighs in defeat and picks up the pace of her walking until she's slightly ahead of me. I think I finally got her to drop it. I hope.

But if I'm being completely honest, I'm dying to let her know everything I feel about her. So why do I keep pushing her away? What if what she wants to say is important? Could this partially ruin our friendship? I hope not.

If my brain would just listen to my heart right now, I would grab her and hug the life out of her. Then I'd kiss the shit out of her if I could.

If.

As I approach the family huddled up on a large picnic blanket Lukas gives me a smirk. He probably thinks I won her over or something. Yeah, I fucking wish.

I sit beside him on the picnic blanket as Ali sits beside Tate. Lukas discreetly hits my arm, giving me a "knowingly" look. "Well? Did you win her over dude?" He whispers.

As I said, I fucking wish.

Ignoring him, I grab a chip that's set in a bowl, plopping it into my mouth. The chip's flavor immediately hits my tongue.

Lukas hits my arm again, looking slightly annoyed this time. "Dude, don't ignore me like that," he whispers again.

That definitely was not my intention.

"Sorry man, what'd you say?" I try playing it off cool, plopping another chip into my mouth. "Don't play dumb, Zayden. Did you win her over or not?" He said, his eyes drifting from me to Ali.

I try playing dumb this time. "Who are we talking about?"

Lukas gives me a "are you fucking stupid look" causing me to quietly laugh. "No, I didn't win her over, no big deal though," I respond, shrugging my shoulders, playing cool as if I don't feel like my body is just going to collapse at any second.

"Bro why?" He asks, looking more interested in this than his math homework.

I shrug again, trying my hardest not to lift my head and look at Ali who is probably looking at me right now.

The beach went by pretty well. I didn't talk to Ali but we did share a few glances and smiles so it didn't look awkward around our families. But it was awkward as shit, and I'm sure some people picked it up.

Aurora definitely did and I could tell. Big sisters always know what's up. Too bad I don't have one to talk to.

We are currently all sitting in the living room, opening Christmas presents. Summer just got all hyped because she got a new iPad.

I got a new Laptop. Thankfully, my other one was old and beginning to glitch and all that recently. It barely worked too.

After everyone received gifts from their families, it was time for the extra gifts lying around. My mom went to pick up one gift from under the tree and her smile became bigger as she read who it was from. "Zayden it's for you," she hands me the wrapped present.

Eyeing the present in my hand carefully, trying to figure out what's under the carefully added wrapping paper.

As I tear apart the wrapping paper, my eyes immediately widen at the gift.

Two identical bracelets with the initials A.G and Z.G. Aliyia Grace and Zayden Gryant? I immediately go to read the note attached on the side.

Thank you for being there for me when I first moved here. I appreciate you so much, and I hope I can show my gratitude with this gift. I know it's not much but I mean, who doesn't like matching bracelets? Anyways, thank you for everything and most of all being my best friend throughout my New York journey. Ew, that sounds so cringe but you get the point :)

-Ali

Ali. This gift is from Ali. She got us matching bracelets. I remember telling her how much I would love to match them with someone sometime. She remembered.

We never spoke about it ever again but she still remembered.

I smile at the gift before lifting my head to meet Ali's eyes. A small smile tugs on her lips, as she tries to hide it with a neutral expression.

I mouth a "thank you" to her and she nods.

My mom goes to grab another gift from the tree and her smile widens again. She places the gift in Ali's hand. I recognize the packaging a little too well.

I bought her that.

It was a small gift but I hope she loves it.

Ali tears the packaging and a necklace box comes into vision. I try to contain my smile, knowing she's probably going to come after me for buying her this after.

She opens the lid of the box, her eyes immediately opening and her jaw-dropping as she stares at the shiny silver metal sitting beneath her.

A silver heart necklace with diamonds sat on the box. Her expression quickly changed from dull to shocked.

"Holy fuck!" She exclaims, placing the necklace in her palm. "Why would you get me this Zayden? The price was insane," she asks facing me, the necklace dangling in her hand.

I shrug it off. I paid a good five hundred and sixty-seven dollars for that necklace. Just praying she doesn't lose it or anything. "It was cheap, you liked it, so why not?"

When the group went to the mall I remember Ali stopping by the jewelry store to window shop. She had her eyes set on this necklace the whole time but was upset because of the price.

So of course, I did what any logical person would do, I went back there as soon as I could and bought her the necklace. I was going to give it to her sooner but then I realized Christmas was a better time.

"Cheap? This necklace was anything but cheap, seriously why'd you get me this Zayden?" Because I like you so much I wouldn't mind spending a whole five hundred dollars (plus tax) on you.

"Because you liked it?" I stand up and sit down next to her, taking the necklace from her hand. "Here, let me put it on."

I wrap the necklace around her neck before booking it from the back. "There"

She pulls out her phone and switches to the camera app, admitting the necklace from the phone view. It looks much better in person but I won't say that out loud.

"Thank you so much Zayden, I love it!" She says, throwing herself at me and wrapping her arms around my body.

She smells so good, oh my.

I return the gesture and wrap my arms around her, patting her back. "You're welcome, Ali." I hear what sounds to be a sigh of relief from her when I call her Ali. Guess she thinks we're back to normal now. I think we are.

I clear my throat remembering that everyone is watching us. She takes that as a hint and pulls herself off me, a smile on her face that she isn't trying to hide.

If I made her happy then there's no reason for me to be upset anymore.

She's happy.

I'm happy.

Authors Note❤❤❤❤

brace ur selves for the next chapter. hint it's the chapter we've all been waiting for. □□□□ it's finally time for me to feed u guys well fr

37 | Official

Z ayden

It's New Year's Eve.

We're about to enter a brand new year in just a few hours. I have so many things I want to let go of and start fresh this upcoming year.

I have one thing set on my New Years' resolution that I hope I can follow through with.

And that is becoming the boyfriend of Aliyia Grace.

Weird but I know what the feeling I've been feeling is now. And though she might not feel the same I'm sure if I keep pushing, maybe she'll someday feel something for me. Whether that takes days or months.

I like Aliyia Grace.

I really do.

And if I could just be her boyfriend right now I would be the happiest man alive.

I look at the bracelet on my hand, the one Ali gave me for Christmas. Ever since I put it on, it hasn't left my hand. Same with the necklace I bought her. It seems like she hasn't taken it off since I put it on her. You don't know how happy that makes me.

"Zayden, just to let you know everyone's meeting downstairs in an hour!" I hear my stepdad's voice from behind the door.

I shout back loud enough in response, "Okay!"

I like my stepdad. A lot.

He's treated me like his biological son ever since the day I met him. We've gotten into arguments and all that but he did what a reasonable father would do. First, they would give their son some space for a while, then they would sit down with them, talk it out and hug it out.

They would not yell at their not even a teenager son telling him he's a "stupid fucking idiot" and all the shit you should never tell a child.

My stepdad has never missed any of my hockey games without a good reason and proof. Yes, he showed proof.

Unlike a certain someone who would never show up to my hockey games and while every child ran up to their parents after a game, I would sit down on the bench because my mother couldn't make it and my father was always absent.

Not that it matters anymore. I don't care anymore.

I don't care because that man is no longer my father. He's no longer the father who made me feel like I was drowning and every time I tried seeking out the top I would plunge deeper into the water into an endless cycle of suffocating.

Anyways.

"Fifteen minutes everyone!" Lukas's dad announces, handing the adults a glass of champagne.

We're all huddled up standing in the living room talking among ourselves while watching the timer on the tv.

Aurora approaches me, her champagne glass being held in one hand. "Zayden, do you have feelings for my sister?"

Oh wow, going straight into it.

I tilt my head trying to keep my eyes from looking at Ali. "Why?"

"Because you look at her a lot, you're always smiley when she's around, you took her and only her to a convenience store and bought her something on Christmas, and you bought her a five hundred dollar necklace she's been wanting for Christmas," she said, her eyes focused on her champagne glass. "Could it be any more obvious?"

Well, I didn't know she was that observant. "And if I do?" I challenge.

"You're making it seem like I'm the overprotective sister," she pauses, taking a swig out of her champagne before speaking. "I don't care at all but just don't hurt her. Respect her boundaries and don't try to push her to do things she doesn't want to do. And I'm being dead serious Zayden, don't fucking hurt her."

"I won't." I respond, my brain only processing half of what she said. "It would hurt me to hurt her."

"Good, that's what I like to hear. Keep that mindset and don't hurt her." Aurora says before walking away to sit and chat with Summer.

I think Summer likes having her around. Probably feels good to have a "sister" for the holidays.

My eyes betray me and drift over to Ali who I catch already staring at me. Once her eyes meet mine she immediately looks somewhere else, avoiding eye contact.

I look at the television to see that there are only ten minutes until the new year. Ten minutes till I can let this year go.

The months of November to December are the best months of this year. Only because Ali came back into my life at those times.

Lukas approaches me, a grin plastered on his face. "So, are you an Aliyia a thing now?" I wish. I shake my head, not meeting his face because I know he'll give me that "bro are you serious?" look.

"Yeah, dude you're fucked. Just go talk to her, tell her your feelings and maybe she'll feel the same. If she doesn't then you can leave it in the past," he continues. "You still got approximately nine minutes and thirty seconds, go make it count."

I look at him, my jaw dropping to the floor. "Did you just say something smart for once?" I question, letting the smile out.

He flips me off and laughs. "Fuck off, now go get 'em tiger," I cringe at the words. Who in their right mind still says "go get 'em, tiger"? Especially someone who is seventeen years old.

"No way you just said that," I cringe, looking at his serious expression. "I was being fucking sarcastic, now take my advice or let yourself drown in the sorrow of not confessing your feelings in the last eight minutes of the year."

Um okay.

I think about it for a second before my body has a mind of its own and is already walking towards Ali.

"Hey," I greet, trying not to show how nervous I am.

"Hi,"

There's no way in hell I could confess to her in front of everyone. Yeah, never. Especially not Summer, she would make fun of me and I would never hear the end of it. "Can we go out the back and talk for a second?"

Her eyes drift from me to her best friend sitting beside us, listening to our conversation. "Um, sure I guess,"

I put my hands in my pocket and make a beeline for the back door, hoping she's following behind me and I'm not just walking out here alone.

When I'm outside I turn around to see Ali standing directly behind me. Good.

"So what's up?" She asks, her fingers playing with the necklace on her neck. That necklace looks beautiful on her. Actually, she looks beautiful with the necklace. No, I lied she looks gorgeous with and without the necklace.

There's no holding back now.

"I'm sorry for kinda lashing out on you Christmas, I don't know why I did it. Actually, I lied, I know why because I like you so much. I like you so much I don't even know what to do with myself anymore, you're all I think about day and night. That kiss meant everything to me even if it was just a kiss to you. I feel so much for you and I guess I was just hoping you felt something for me too."

I can't believe I just said all that in one breath. I watch her expression closely, waiting for anything that could mean a sign of rejection.

But instead, I get a warm smile. A smile.

She just smiled at my words and now my heart is doing jumping jacks.

She doesn't say anything though, she just smiles. It's kinda worrying me. "Are you going to say something?" I ask, feeling slightly embarrassed now.

"Zayden," she starts, the smile on her face not leaving. "I was so unsure about my feelings but now I understand them. I like you so much too, and it's been in my head ever since Christmas. I wanted to tell you I felt something for you too but you kept cutting me off and I thought it was best not to."

Great, now I feel stupid for not letting her finish what she planned to say. Nothing else slips from my mouth other than a simple "oh".

She reaches out to cup both sides of my face, her smile growing bigger at the second. "I feel lots of things for you and you don't know how happy it makes me knowing you feel the same," she tells me before leaning in.

And she kisses me.

She fucking kisses me.

I pull away from the kiss first, wanting to get a quick look at her face before pulling her back in by her waist. Her hands move from my cheeks to wrapping around my neck.

Her lips move in a smooth slow rhythm against mine. And I keep myself in control before I feel her smile against my lips.

Holy fuck.

I don't stop kissing her but I do manage to slip a few words out. "You drive me crazy."

She really does.

"I know," is all that she says while she continues kissing me.

As much as I want to continue kissing her, I still want to talk to her. I pull away my lips but keep my hands on her waist. "So what you're saying is you like me back?"

She nods, her eyes remaining on mine.

I can't help but smile. This has been my dream for over a month now. And my dream is finally coming to reality.

Her hands move to my hair, her fingers running through them so softly. "So what are we going to do about this, huh?"

Option one, I can make her my girlfriend.

Option two, she can make me her boyfriend.

I pull her closer to me, trying my hardest not to fall back into her lips again. "You could let me be your boyfriend?"

"I could."

"You should."

She tilts her head, giggling a little. "Should I?"

I nod, not wanting anything else in the world right now than her.

She makes a humming sound as if she's thinking about it. "Alright then say it,"

"Say what exactly?"

"Say it. Say you want to be my boyfriend. Ask me."

Sounds demanding but I'll allow it. Anything for her.

"Can I be your boyfriend?"

Her eyes brighten and her smile widens. "What's the magic word?"

She's trying to make me beg now... I like it.

"Can I be your boyfriend, please?" I add, wanting to hear her approval.

"Hmm under one condition," she holds her pointer finger in the air. One condition? I'm not sure what it is but it's already terrifying.

I tilt my head, waiting for her to elaborate.

"We keep it a secret for a while," she elaborates.

What? I don't think I can do that. That means I can't show was a boyfriend would do in public. Only in private? What if other guys flirt with her? I might lose my shit.

"No." I deadpan, not wanting her to elaborate anymore.

"Yes, or it isn't happening."

"That's so not fair."

"It's fair to me, Zayden. Please? I'll still be your girlfriend either way."

Yes, that is true but, that means I wouldn't get to show her off. Wouldn't get to show everyone that I got her and they didn't. Because I'm simply better than everyone else, except Ali. I think she's the only person better than me.

"A secret from who exactly?" I ask, needing confirmation if I can tell my best friend about all of this.

"Everyone."

"Including Tate and Lukas?" I mean, they are our best friends they deserve to know:

She nods, letting her hands fall to her sides. Aw too bad, I missed having them in my hair.

I would do it for her but it would take everything in me not to just kiss her in front of everyone. And it's going to kill me having to pretend that we're just friends.

But it will also feel good because then we know things everyone else doesn't. We know the bond we share when it's just the two of us. I could live with that.

I let out a sigh, wanting her to be my girlfriend right now. "Alright."

"Okay so now we're officially boyfriend and girlfriend!" She whispered but I could still hear the excitement in her voice.

I held eye contact with her, the biggest smiles ever on both hers and my face. Her eyes were so captivating, by far one of her most attractive features.

My grip on her waist tightened as I drew her closer to me, desperate to feel her lips on mine again. I leaned in and kissed her.

And of course, she immediately kissed me back, as eager as I am. I think her lips are part of the top three most captivating things about her.

Everything about her is just, Woah.

She makes my heart do gymnastics like crazy, without even allowing my heart to stretch either.

All she has to do is just stand there and I'm already feeling my heart twist and turn. Every second we're together I wish we could just be together forever, but eventually, everyone leaves.

That's not me and Ali tho, I'm convinced we are immortal and nothing can change my mind.

Ali's hands find their way back to wrap around my neck, drawing herself as close to me as possible.

And just as we're enjoying our second nighttime kiss, we hear "Happy New Year" coming from inside the house, along with Fireworks that have just begun to go off.

My head lifts up to catch a look at the fireworks. Fireworks are so pretty. I enjoy watching them every time. But this time I want all my focus to be on her.

Ali looks up at the sky, a warm smile plastered on her face. "Happy new year, Zayden."

My goodness could she be any more pretty?

"Happy new year, Ali." I pull her in for another slow soft kiss as the fireworks above us shoot loud crackling noises.

This is just perfect.

She's perfect.

"I don't think you knew how much I liked you," I tell her against her lips.

"Oh yeah? Tell me more."

I grin and continue kissing her, not elaborating any further.

Everything I've ever wanted.

I think it's safe to say I am the happiest man alive right now.

Definitely.

Lightning Source UK Ltd.
Milton Keynes UK
UKHW020750260123
416005UK00015B/753